Fall to Pieces

A Southern Quilting Mystery, Volume 7

Elizabeth Craig

Published by Elizabeth Craig, 2017.

FALL TO PIECES

First edition. January 17, 2017.

Written by Elizabeth Craig.

For Riley and Elizabeth Ruth

Chapter One

"I know a secret!"

Beatrice stared wearily at her friend. She hoped Meadow didn't expect her to play a guessing game. Beatrice was already running a little behind with her day. Having Meadow drop by with her tremendous dog wasn't helping her get caught up. She carefully moved her foot away when she saw that Boris's mouth was open and a wad of drool looked as if it might fall at any moment.

Meadow, red glasses slightly askew and gray hairs coming out of her long braid, gave Beatrice an impatient look as if she were falling down on her end. "Don't you want to know what it is?"

Beatrice's corgi, Noo-noo, gave her a concerned look and nudged Beatrice with her nose. She was hoping that Beatrice could escort their visitors out so that she and Beatrice could resume their lovely nap.

Beatrice knew that Meadow would end up spilling her secret any second. One thing in life was certain: Meadow Downey could not keep a secret. It would eat her alive.

Sure enough, Meadow had a mini-explosion and reached out to grab Beatrice's arm. "Promise you won't say anything to anybody?" Seeing Beatrice's consenting nod, Meadow said, "Oh Beatrice! My Ash is going to ask your Piper to marry him. Isn't it wonderful? And you and I will be related!"

Beatrice felt a warm glow course through her. It was indeed good news. She knew her daughter loved Meadow's son and was happy that Ash wanted to spend his life with Piper. Better yet, Ash had moved to North Carolina so Piper would be staying in Dappled Hills.

"How is it, though," asked Beatrice, "that you and I know about this proposal before Piper? Doesn't that seem a little backward?"

"Not really," said Meadow in a casual way. "Ash asked for my help."

Beatrice blinked at her. "Excuse me?"

"My *help*," said Meadow a bit louder, in case Beatrice was becoming hard of hearing.

Beatrice tilted her head to one side. "Why on earth would Ash need your help with a proposal? This isn't some sort of Cyrano de Bergerac type of thing, is it? You don't need to feed a script to Ash, do you?"

"Of *course* not! As if Ash couldn't come up with his own wording of his proposal. For heaven's sake, Beatrice! But it's clear that you don't know about modern proposal culture. Proposals now are *events*. There are all these incredibly creative and fabulous ways to ask someone to marry you. Ash needed a little help from us to make this meaningful for Piper," said Meadow.

"From *me*, too?" Beatrice was rather horrified. "But I wouldn't want to be part of something very personal for Piper. I'd think that Ash would just pop the question."

"And she'd probably say no to such a revoltingly boring proposal!" scoffed Meadow.

"We're not going to *be* there, but we're going to help out. Ash wants to make his proposal part of a quilt—a future heirloom. And he wants our loving hands making it for it to be especially special," said Meadow.

"I see," said Beatrice slowly. And, thinking of it, it did sound like a lovely idea. Piper would be very touched to think that so much thought and time went into his proposal.

"As you can imagine, I need your help," said Meadow briskly. "She reached down and patted Boris, which made his drool production increase significantly.

"Of course," said Beatrice. "Should we go to the quilt shop to take a look at some possibilities?"

"First things first," said Meadow, producing a notebook and a pen. "I want to get everything exactly right. What are Piper's favorite colors?"

Beatrice shook her head. "I've no idea."

"What about her favorite quotations or maybe part of a favorite song?" asked Meadow, pen hovering expectantly over the notebook.

"I'm not really sure," said Beatrice with a shrug.

Meadow snapped her notebook closed. "What kind of a mother are you?" she demanded. "I suppose you're going to have to be a detective again and uncover some clues that we can use to make this quilt beautiful for Piper. Then maybe you can contribute a few squares to the project. I'm really going to try to power through this—maybe pull an all-nighter. And I could use your help in keeping Piper's schedule free so that Ash can actually pop the question."

Beatrice, who'd gotten a good book lately from Meadow's husband, Ramsay, stifled a sigh. "I can see my quiet afternoons of reading in the hammock with Noo-noo drifting away," she said dryly.

"Phooey. When do you ever sit still longer than fifteen minutes, despite your best intentions? You'll probably get more relaxation time by scheduling more things to do," said Meadow, standing up. She stopped short, staring across the room. "What on earth is that?"

"That's a plant," said Beatrice, hearing a defensive edge creep into her voice.

"*Is* it?" asked Meadow doubtfully. "It looks as if it needs to be on life support."

Beatrice glanced over at the philodendron. Its trailing stems looked dry and stressed. "You know that I always have a problem keeping houseplants alive. I have a lot better luck with everything outside."

"I'm sure your outdoor plants are grateful for that!" said Meadow fervently. "I'm surprised you keep trying to sustain life indoors, considering the victims of your experiments."

"This was a gift from Wyatt," said Beatrice with a sigh. "I tried hard, but the harder I tried, the sicklier it got."

Wyatt and Beatrice had been seeing each other for a while. Beatrice loved their dinners and picnics and listening to him preach at church on Sundays. But somehow he'd never really picked up on the message that she wasn't wonderful with houseplants.

Meadow surveyed the plant, hands on her hips. "Would you mind if I took it with me? I can try to give it CPR once I get back home. Then, if I can nurse it back to health, you can take it back home."

"Meadow, you've got a deal," said Beatrice, feeling relieved. She paused. "Now what were we talking about?"

"How you can relax better by adding more to your schedule," said Meadow

absently, still critically studying the plant. She walked over briskly and picked it up, making a face.

"How do you figure that?" asked Beatrice.

"Because you'll genuinely be tired! And less restless," said Meadow.

"I can see your point, although I don't think this quilt is exactly going to use up all my free time."

"Which is why Posy's upcoming activities are so perfect for you," said Meadow.

"Posy's upcoming activities?" echoed Beatrice weakly. Posy was the quilt shop owner and another friend of Beatrice's.

"Exactly. She'll explain everything at the quilt shop. I'm going to encourage the entire guild to get involved. Posy has always been such a good friend to the Village Quilters," said Meadow.

"Let's head over there now. We can pick up some materials for Piper's quilt and can talk to Posy about her plans at the same time."

"What about Boris?" asked Beatrice as the giant beast stuck his tongue out at her, grinning.

"Let's stuff him in your car and drop him and your plant off at my house before we go. That will give you the opportunity to call Piper and ask some nonchalant questions about her favorite colors," said Meadow, heading for the door, holding the leash with one hand and awkwardly balancing the plant on her hip with the other.

"How on earth is someone nonchalant about favorite colors?" muttered Beatrice as she grabbed her purse and gave Noo-noo a soothing pat.

"Oh, you know. Just say you were thinking about painting your living room or something and you wondered what Piper's favorite colors were," said Meadow absently as Boris lunged forward, jerking her behind him.

"Don't you want me to hold the plant for you?" asked Beatrice, watching as it bobbled on Meadow's hip.

"Certainly not! Don't you think you've done enough damage to it?" said Meadow with a sniff.

Beatrice gave up arguing about both the plant and the favorite color conversation, realizing when there was no way out. She started dialing Piper as Meadow and Boris clambered into her sedan. She put the window down and Boris immediately stuck his massive head outside it, continuing to grin.

As usual, the sound of her daughter's voice made Beatrice smile. Beatrice had retired to the village of Dappled Hills after many years as an art curator in Atlanta to be near her Piper, who taught school here and lived close by.

"Hi Piper," said Beatrice.

"Oh, hi, Mama!" said Piper. "I was just about to call you."

"Really? Did you need me for something?" asked Beatrice as she started up the car. She put the phone on speaker. Meadow mouthed *colors* at her.

"Well, I was just going to ask you something, that's all. I'm definitely not trying to fill up your calendar, because I know how you're trying to keep it fairly light. You *are* retired, after all," said Piper.

"I am, although being quiet doesn't always turn out that way," said Beatrice, giving Meadow a baleful look. "You know that I'm always open to doing things with *you*, though."

Meadow, who could hear the conversation, since it was on speaker, mouthed: *no! Ash needs time, too!*

"I was just trying to see what your next week looks like so that I can maybe plan a lunch or come by with a supper or at least have a coffee or something," said Piper. "Do you have your calendar in front of you?"

"Oh, I don't think my schedule is full enough for me to have to look at the calendar," said Beatrice. "Actually it looks pretty open." In fact, it didn't, but this wasn't the time to go into that. "I've got a quilt to work on, but that can be at any time."

"Okay, great!" said Piper, sounding happy. "I'll get back to you then and we'll set something up. Was there something that you needed to ask me?"

"To ask you?" repeated Beatrice, turning into Meadow's driveway.

Meadow became very animated beside her, which excited Boris for some unknown reason and he barked.

"Is that Noo-noo?" asked Piper, a concerned note in her voice. "She sounds like she has a cold."

"Oh, it's just Meadow and Boris, popping by," said Beatrice. "It's ... well, I was thinking of painting my living room and I was trying to decide on a color."

"Really? You just painted when you moved here. And I know how much you hate painting. I thought you said at the time that you'd never paint your house again. The paint kept dripping on your clothes and it was hard to paint in the corners and where the walls met the ceiling. And you had everything covered with drop cloths and furniture still somehow managed to get a little paint on it."

Meadow was shaking her head and mouthing: *colors!*

"Maybe it's just my restless nature, always looking for a project," said Beatrice mildly.

"I hear you on the restless part, but I don't recall your looking for a project," said Piper. "Is everything okay?"

"Perhaps I'm just looking for a change. What *are* your favorite colors, by the way? Out of curiosity? Not still different shades of pink, I'm guessing? I think those were the last favorites of yours that I was aware of," said Beatrice, clearing her throat a bit at the end. "And that was when you wanted to be a ballerina when you grew up."

"No, not pink. You mean favorite colors in *general*? Not favorite colors to wear? Because I love to wear black, but I sure don't like to decorate with it."

"Right. I mean favorite colors in general," said Beatrice. Her eyes glared daggers into Meadow's back as she took Boris inside.

"Probably yellow and light blue. They're cheerful. Sometimes cheerful is nice, "said Piper. She sounded just the slightest bit wary, as if she were becoming a little concerned at the odd trajectory of their conversation.

"Okay. Good to know. I'll take that under advisement," said Beatrice hastily as Meadow started walking back toward the car. She wanted to wrap the conversation up before Meadow started orchestrating it again.

"And I'll get back to you soon and we can plan a time to get together," said Piper cheerfully. "Talk to you later."

Meadow, slightly winded from having Boris pull her around before she'd gotten him inside, said, "So, did you get the info?"

"Yellow and blue," said Beatrice. "And my daughter likely thinks I'm losing it."

"Everything will be clear once she is Ash's fiancée," said Meadow, waving a hand dismissively. "What about the other stuff?"

Beatrice frowned as she backed the car out of the driveway. "Other stuff?"

"You didn't remember to ask about the favorite quotation or poem?" asked Meadow. "Now *I* think you're losing it."

"These subjects hardly fall under the category of casual conversation. I'll bring up the other things the next time I talk to her. It sounds like we're meeting up soon and maybe I can fit it in the conversation more naturally," said Beatrice with a sigh.

"Good. Then I can take the quotations and the lines of poetry and integrate them into the quilt along with the pictures that Ash gives me," said Meadow. "And I'm going to leave the most important part to you!"

"What's that?" asked Beatrice warily.

"The proposal itself, of course! You do lovely machine work and you have that amazing new sewing machine. If Piper's favorite colors are yellow and blue, you can embroider maybe a dark-blue framed block with *Piper, will you marry me?* on it." Meadow teared up at the end of the sentence and fished a tissue out of the pocket of her long, multi-colored skirt. "I think it would be just fine to machine embroider," she added gruffly.

Beatrice felt touched, herself. "So just embroider *Piper, will you marry me* on a square?"

"Oh, maybe surround the words with flowers or hearts or something. Something pretty and sweet. You know what to do—you always do such a good job with everything. But it's the most important part!" stressed Meadow again. "We'll pick up everything we need at Posy's."

They arrived at the quilt shop a couple of minutes later. Posy's Patchwork Cottage was the only quilt store in the area and usually drew quite a few regional quilters to her carefully collected fabrics and notions. This time it looked a bit quieter than usual. Beatrice and Meadow pushed open the cheerful red door to the cheery chime of the bell. As usual, it was a peaceful spot in the quiet town. Lilting bluegrass music was playing softly in the background, gingham curtains blew in the breeze from the open windows. And lovely fabrics in all sorts of designs provided pops of color. Quilts hung everywhere: from the ceilings, on the walls, and over antique sewing machines and washstands.

Posy smiled warmly at them as they came in and gave them both hugs. She said, "I'm so glad y'all are here!" As was usual, she was wearing a fluffy cardigan sweater with a butterfly brooch on the shoulder. Her blue eyes shone behind a small pair of glasses.

Meadow grinned broadly at her. "It's great to be wanted. Our stunning looks and amazing personalities, I'm sure." She walked over to the sitting area in the middle of the store and plopped down on a soft sofa with a gingham slipcover. Beatrice sat across from her in a comfy armchair. Maisy the shop cat jumped up on the arm of the sofa next to Meadow and proceeded to have a bath.

"Those too! But I mostly wanted to tap into your clever minds. I'm looking for ideas for getting quilters to spend some more time here." Posy sat next to Meadow on the sofa. "Meadow recommended that I schedule some more activities here."

Meadow said, "Everyone loves the Patchwork Cottage! They're here all the time. Except, maybe, lately."

"Thanks, Meadow!" said Posy, her eyes twinkling at the compliment. "They do run in to shop and everyone is very supportive. In fact, they're *so* supportive that I want to do something nice for them in return."

Beatrice said, "You always have events here, though. You do a lot for quilters."

"But I think I need to focus more on my core group of customers. Most of the events I've given lately have been focused on reaching out to new quilters and introducing folks to the craft," said Posy.

Meadow clapped her hands together in excitement, startling Maisie, who put her ears back and shot Meadow a baleful look. "I know! I've got an idea! I heard from a quilting cousin of mine who lives on the other side of the country that her guild was hosting a 'Sew and Tell.' They meet up to work on their quilts and tell everyone what they've been up to and show their latest projects— like a *show* and tell in school, but a *Sew* and Tell."

"That does sound like fun," said Posy enthusiastically. "I could decorate the back room with quilts and notions and bring in some hors d'oeuvres and punch."

Beatrice said, "I'd be sure to also display your newest fabrics and maybe offer some sort of discount or coupon for bulk purchases to encourage more spending. Another idea for your veteran quilters that might be fun is a mystery quilt. That could be something different that would appeal to an experienced quilter."

Meadow gave an approving gasp at the idea. "Oh! I *love* mystery quilts. It's so much fun to work on a project without knowing what it will look like in the end."

"What are you working on now, Meadow?" asked Posy. "I always love hearing all about your projects."

Meadow, who not only was a terrible secret-keeper, but a very truthful person, turned bright red. Her eyes cut across desperately to Beatrice.

"It's a collaborative effort," said Beatrice smoothly stepping in. "Meadow and I are going to work on a quilt together. We're still ironing out the details."

Posy nodded absently, staring with great curiosity at the speechless Meadow. Beatrice couldn't blame her. A tongue-tied Meadow was an unusual sight.

"Anyway," said Beatrice briskly, "I think the Sew and Tell and the mystery quilt might be just the ticket to keep more experienced quilters engaged. Has it ... well, has it been a little quieter in the Patchwork Cottage lately, too?"

Posy nodded. "Oh, nothing that I'd want to complain about."

Meadow said staunchly, "You're never one to complain, anyway!"

Posy smiled at her. "I don't know about that, but thanks. And the Village Quilters have been absolutely wonderful, as usual, about coming in. They're all so committed to their craft and so supportive of me."

"But the Cut-Ups?" asked Beatrice. "That guild hasn't been in as much lately?"

"They've been a little quiet," admitted Posy. "Their traffic has just dropped off a bit."

Meadow frowned. "Come to think of it, I've noticed they haven't been very active lately. They haven't been well-represented at any of the recent quilt shows, for instance. I wonder what's going on with them?"

"I don't really know them very well," said Beatrice. "Of course I've met some of them and might be able to come up with their names if I had to. Who are some of the quieter Cut-Ups that I might not know as well?"

The bell on the wooden door chimed and a middle-aged woman with graying hair pulled rather severely back walked in. She glanced hesitantly around her and then gave a tight smile as Posy hurried up.

"Henrietta!" said Posy cheerfully. "It's so good to see you. Can I help you to find something? We've got some lovely new fabrics in."

As Posy and Henrietta walked toward the other side of the shop, Meadow leaned in and said in her loudest stage whisper, "Henrietta is one of them."

Chapter Two

"One of whom?" asked Beatrice.

"One of the Cut-Ups," said Meadow impatiently. "What we were just talking about."

"I think I recognize her," said Beatrice slowly. "I'm not sure, though. You'd think in a town as small as this one that I'd have met everyone. Especially a quilter."

Meadow threw up her hands, startling Maisie the cat, which very coldly rose and pointedly stalked over to sit in Beatrice's lap. "Some of these women are just not out and about as much as they should be. They need to participate more and be part of the art festivals and quilt shows and different quilting service projects. The fact you haven't met even *one* of them is scandalous. Just scandalous, Beatrice."

Beatrice put a finger in front of her lips, giving Meadow a look. Meadow had a habit of getting louder as she got more agitated. "Then it sounds like Posy is on to something. Get some of the older, more experienced quilters more engaged by creating events especially for them. Make them feel part of the quilting community. And I'll add, although Posy didn't mention it, have them spend more at the shop."

"There's got to be other things we can do to bring folks in," fretted Meadow. "Posy doesn't seem to do any marketing at all, you know."

Beatrice asked, "Does she have an email list?"

"Email *list*? She has an *email*. Is that the same?"

"No, I'm talking about a list of emails for her regular customers. That way she can send out specials for quilters or give them rewards or coupons or newsletters—that kind of thing," said Beatrice. "Incentives for giving her their email addresses. We maintained those types of lists at the museum when I was the curator there."

Meadow said, "Well, it certainly sounds like something she needs to start doing, if she doesn't already. I don't think I've ever gotten an email from the shop, come to think of it. And I sure wouldn't mind coupons. You know Ramsay. He always makes these horrid clucking sounds when he balances the checkbook register."

"That mystery quilt should be a good way to start collecting emails. The important thing is that the customer knows they're signing up to receive newsletters or marketing or whatever. Maybe the mystery quilt could be the enticement for them to voluntarily sign up to be on the list," said Beatrice. She stroked Maisie and the purring cat lifted her chin to allow Beatrice better access.

Meadow beamed at her. "Genius! Now, if only you'd put that brain to use by trying to figure out what Piper's favorite poem or song verses are."

Beatrice was eager to change the subject. In a low voice she said, "Going back to our conversation. Was Henrietta involved in the quilting community before?"

"Oh, certainly! That is to say ... well. I don't suppose she was ever at its center or anything. She's much more of a periphery person. She's rather quiet and not extremely social. What little she has done socially has all been connected to quilting. And she's an excellent quilter, I think. She does some experimental stuff." Meadow frowned. "We'll have to reach out to all the Henriettas of Dappled Hills and get them more involved."

This sounded like one of those statements that people make and then don't really follow-up on, so Beatrice started a bit when Meadow bellowed, "Henrietta!"

The reaching-out process was immediate with Meadow.

A wide-eyed Henrietta appeared from around a rack of notions. "Yes? Oh, hello, Meadow."

Meadow briskly introduced Henrietta and Beatrice and then said, "I was just telling Beatrice here that we haven't been seeing nearly as much of the Cut-Ups around and about as we used to. We used to have such fun together! What's happening?"

Henrietta colored a little, perhaps feeling called out by Meadow. "Yes we did. Well, you know, everyone is just so busy and everything."

"Busy with *quilting* is what we should be," said Meadow emphatically. "And Posy, Beatrice, and I have ideas about how to get busier."

Posy, hearing her name, walked over while Beatrice winced at the thought of becoming busier than she already was.

"First thing is a Sew and Tell where we can all brag about our latest projects and get some ideas for future quilts by hearing about everyone else's," said Meadow. "We'll also be working on mystery quilts, which will be fun. We can all make guesses as to what the finished quilt will end up looking like."

"And I already have an idea for it," said Posy, looking excited.

Henrietta nodded and asked, "When is the Sew and Tell?"

"Right away!" said Meadow. Then she looked across at Posy. "That is, if Posy can host it quickly."

Posy smiled at her. "I'm sure I could pull it together."

Beatrice said, "I'll help you, Posy. It sounds as if it's a matter of just coordinating food and drinks and clearing the room a bit."

"And contacting everyone," reminded Meadow. "That will be the most important part. Except that Posy doesn't have everyone's email."

Henrietta cleared her throat. "I could let the Cut-Ups know. I've got their emails."

Meadow said, "For that matter, *I* even have most of the Cut-Ups emails. Let's say it will be next Friday night." She glanced up at Posy and got a nodding confirmation. "Why not just start in right away?"

Beatrice had the feeling that she needed to have her calendar in front of her. Then she remembered. "What time, though? I think I'm supposed to have dinner with Wyatt that night. Or maybe it's actually *this* Friday that I'm supposed to."

"Oh, there will be *plenty* of time to have dinner with Wyatt," said Meadow. "Even if it's next Friday, you could always go after the Sew and Tell is over."

Henrietta said, "Early would be good for me. I'm not great at driving at night anymore."

"So maybe five o'clock?" asked Posy. Maisie the cat jumped up to bound over to Posy and rub lovingly against her legs.

Beatrice said, "That should work out."

"It does sound like fun," said Henrietta. "I haven't done anything with other quilters for a while."

Meadow said, "It's the perfect opportunity! Then you can show off what you're working on now." She gushed to Beatrice, "Henrietta is a very talented quilter. I can't wait to see what she's working on now."

"I haven't even started yet," protested Henrietta with a small smile. "That's what I'm here today for."

"Now you have plenty of time to really get going on it before we have our event," said Meadow smoothly. "And it will be nice to have Beatrice there, too. Beatrice is a relatively new quilter, but has really fit right into the quilting culture. I think she's inspirational."

Beatrice flushed as she usually did when Meadow got carried away.

Henrietta said, "Well, count me in. And now I guess I'd better go check out."

"Oh! We also need your email address, Henrietta," said Meadow. "For the mystery quilt, remember?"

Henrietta gave her the email address, paid, and then left.

Meadow said, "At least we've got Henrietta committed. She's great, Beatrice—so, so creative."

"Hasn't she been doing some sort of interior design work?" asked Posy.

Meadow said, "She has. On top of her quilting! Well, it's not *exactly* interior design. It's sort of redesign and reimagine. She takes clients' old things and changes them around to make them look new and exciting."

Beatrice said, "I see. So she rearranges furniture, paints wood, re-covers chairs, that kind of thing."

Meadow said, "That's right. It's been something Henrietta has been doing for the last couple of years. And now she's onboard with the Sew and Tell, too."

Posy said, "You're both so smart! Fingers crossed that this will prove a success. I already have ideas for the quilt, so I can start right away sending instructions out." Then she frowned. "Of course, I won't be able to really start immediately, though, will I? Not without more email addresses. I should have been collecting those all along."

"We'll make up for lost time," said Beatrice. "Meadow said that she already has many email addresses. Maybe she can send out an email on your behalf, letting everyone know about the Sew and Tell and about the mystery quilt."

Meadow added, "And we can put a note on the shop door telling everyone about the different events. Oh, and hand out flyers at the quilt show on Friday. And I may remind everyone that it's not too late to be *part* of the quilt show on Friday. This is going to be so great, Posy!"

It did start out being as great as Meadow thought it would be. Meadow sent out a recruitment email for the quilt show and Posy had lots of signups for the mystery quilt as well as an RSVP for the Sew and Tell.

The first email that Posy sent out to the group told everyone what to buy for the quilt and some introductory instructions.

Beatrice called Wyatt. She realized when she saw her calendar that she'd accepted his invitation for dinner on Friday without understanding that the quilt show might affect her evening.

She smiled when she heard his voice on the phone. Beatrice was happy in Dappled Hills for a number of reasons: she loved being near her daughter and loved the friends she'd made. And she loved being close to Wyatt. She still felt that between all her activities (many of which she felt dragged into) and Wyatt's duties as minister of Dappled Hills Presbyterian Church, they had to work hard to find time to spend together.

"How are you?" asked Wyatt, his voice warm and kind as he answered the phone.

"Great! Except that I seem to be caught up in a whirlwind of quilting activities," said Beatrice ruefully. "I'm calling about dinner on Friday."

Wyatt said, "Need to cancel?"

"No, I think we just need to push our reservation out by thirty minutes. I forgot when we scheduled that I'm at a quilt show that afternoon. I hope that doesn't interfere with our plans too much," said Beatrice.

Wyatt's voice was tinged with relief. "That sounds perfect. I thought you might need to cancel and I'd been looking forward to our dinner. This week has been busy, especially on my end, and I'm glad we get a chance to catch up."

"Can't wait," Beatrice said with a smile.

After they ended their conversation, Beatrice sighed, looking absently at her phone. She knew Meadow was going to continue bugging her about Piper's favorite poetry or verse or whatever. She simply wasn't sure that she was going to be able to subtly get that information without Piper being suspicious that something was behind her request. Or, perhaps, Piper would be suspicious that her mother was losing her mind.

Beatrice cleared her throat as she dialed Piper's number. When Piper answered, she said, "Hi, sweetie!"

"Hi, Mom! How are you?"

"I'm well! Yes, I'm doing well." Beatrice paused. Maybe she should have had her speech prepared before she called. She sounded just a wee bit too perky, to her ears.

"All ready for the quilt show?" asked Piper.

"Not totally, but I'm working on it. You know Meadow—sometimes she creates distractions. Which reminds me; there's going to be a Sew and Tell event at the Patchwork Cottage and a mystery quilt project that you might want to know about or maybe sign up for." Suddenly, she got a mental image of Meadow wagging a finger at her. Wasn't she supposed to help Piper free up her time so that Ash could propose?

"Oh, okay. Thanks! I'm not sure if I have the time for both of them, but I'll think about it. Things have been revving up at school lately: there's parent night coming up and a fundraiser for the PTA. But I'll take a look." She paused. "How is the painting coming?"

"Painting?" asked Beatrice blankly.

"Did you decide on yellow? Or another color?"

Beatrice suddenly remembered that she was supposed to be planning on painting her living room. "Oh! Well, I think I've decided that maybe I didn't have time after all to tackle that right now. But I've made a note of your input for later on. Yellow and light blue. Lovely."

Piper said, "So...were you calling to let me know about the quilt events, or did you just call to chat?"

Beatrice stifled a sigh. She wasn't good at being surreptitious. She definitely hadn't missed her calling as a spy. She said, slowly, "Actually, I wanted your opinion on something. I was thinking about doing a quilt with a phrase or a lyric or a bit of poetry."

Piper's voice was surprised. "Are you? I hadn't gotten the impression that you were interested in quilting those. I thought they might be too modern for your tastes. They sound more like something that *I* might do."

"Yes, well. Sometimes it's good to try something different to keep abreast of what's current in the craft," said Beatrice. "I was curious to hear if you had any ideas of favorite phrases or words. Just as an idea." She stopped and then added quickly, "I have a new machine and wanted to try out the embroidery on it."

"I'd think it would need to be something very short," said Piper thoughtfully. "Otherwise, it might overwhelm the quilt."

"Right. Do you have a favorite poem, for instance?" Beatrice rolled her eyes at Noo-noo as the corgi looked sympathetically at her. This prying all felt very unnatural.

"I don't think my favorites would make for very good quilting," said Piper dryly. "I'm fond of "The Lady of Shalott," and "The Raven," by Poe."

Piper was right. Those wouldn't work for a proposal quilt at all.

Piper continued, "Why don't you try something a little less challenging, Mama? Maybe just *one* word."

"Such as?"

"*Love.* Or *peace.* Something like that," said Piper.

Much better. "I think you're right, Piper. Sometimes I set out to do something a little *too* ambitious. Keeping it simple will work better for me, for sure."

"Glad I could help, Mama."

The day was fairly productive. But then, Thursday night, the evening before the quilt show, there was another email to the mystery quilt list. And it wasn't about the project.

Chapter Three

As soon as Beatrice spotted the email in her inbox, her phone started ringing. It was a breathless Meadow. "Did you get that email?" she demanded. "That dreadful, awful email?"

"I sure did," said Beatrice. "And I know Posy didn't send it."

"She's so upset," said Meadow. "The email is from her address, you know. She's on her way over from the shop to talk with Ramsay and me. Want to come by?"

She was already heading out the door.

If Posy were upset by the email, Meadow's was a good place to go to cheer up. Meadow's home was a converted barn with soaring ceilings scattered with skylights illuminating the exposed rafters and posts. Quilts covered nearly every surface and hung from the walls. Beatrice's favorites were Meadow's crazy quilts which definitely seemed at home in the barn. What was more inviting, Meadow always had something delicious cooking on the stove. The entire effect was one of cozy comfort. And in that cozy comfort, Beatrice couldn't help but notice that the philodendron that Meadow was rehabilitating was looking much perkier already. Beatrice sighed.

Posy was indeed upset. Although, Meadow seemed even more upset than she was. And perhaps she'd dressed after getting the email because her attire was even more mismatched than usual: a riot of reds and hot pinks and turquoise. "It's just such an ugly thing to have done," she steamed as she pulled a cheesy quiche out of the oven. "And with Posy doing so much for quilting in Dappled Hills! Imagine!"

Meadow's husband, Ramsay, police chief for Dappled Hills said calmly to the anxious-looking Posy, "I certainly wouldn't take it personally. Someone is clearly upset with Henrietta and wanted to convey that message to the general public. Your email list was just a convenient means to an end." His whole presence was calming. Instead of his uniform, he was wearing a flannel, plaid shirt with red suspenders stretching over his well-fed stomach. His eyes were kind behind his reading glasses.

Posy blinked rapidly before saying sadly, "I hope you're right, Ramsay. I'd hate to think that anyone would believe that I could be capable of sending out an email like this. And it was supposed to be so fun—our mystery quilt."

"Well, it's surely turned out to be a mystery, all right," said Beatrice in a wry voice. "Posy, you can't believe that anyone would think you could have something to do with this. Even the tone of the email sounds nothing like you. *Henrietta Hunnicutt is lying scum. She should watch her back.*"

Meadow, wielding a knife, sliced murderously into the quiche and throwing slices onto plates in a manner that made Boris the dog drool and edge closer to them.

Posy shivered from hearing the text of the email again and asked, "But how did they do it? How did they make it look like the email was coming from me?"

Ramsay said dryly, "It doesn't help that you've got your email login and password on the wall where everyone checks out. I've noticed that before while waiting for Meadow to wrap up her shopping. It didn't take a hacker to send an email on your behalf."

"There's got to be a way to find out who did it!" said Meadow angrily. "I know I've seen on television where the police track down computers. You need to do that, Ramsay."

"You mean by tracking the IP address? I'll see how far I get with that, but I suspect that whoever was smart enough to log in as Posy was smart enough to use a public computer somewhere. Like the library's computer," said Ramsay.

"Disgusting!" spat Meadow as she violently shoved plates, forks, and napkins at them. "And, what's more, how upsetting to poor Henrietta! She's done nothing to deserve this. She's just a quiet little mouse who rarely even gets involved in anything!"

Ramsay tilted his head to one side. "Are you really sure about that? Sometimes people aren't exactly what they seem."

This statement made Meadow even more irritated. "Of *course*, I'm sure. She's simply a mild-mannered quilter, for heaven's sake. She probably spends her free time watching game shows on television as she works on her next project. She's hardly some sort of nasty gossip going around spreading filth about *other quilters*."

Ramsay, accustomed to Meadow's staunch defense of anything concerning quilting, said, "Okay, well, I'm going to change into my uniform and head out. I'll speak with her and make sure she's okay. I might also try to get a little information about who she thinks might be this upset with her."

"Someone certainly is," said Beatrice. "And it sounds as if Henrietta might be a gossip." She ignored the exasperated sigh from Meadow.

Posy's forehead wrinkled. "I can't even imagine. She's always been so quiet and sweet to me when she comes in the store."

"Yes, but you don't *do* anything for her to gossip about, Posy," said Beatrice. "Maybe she's different when someone she knows has a secret."

Ramsay said, "Nobody in a small town wants their secret out. There's nothing like having the whole town know everything about you. All right, so here's what we're going to do. Posy, you're going to send out an email apologizing for the nastygram everyone received in their inbox, but explaining that it had nothing to do with you. I'll poke around a little and see what I find—and also hope nothing else happens. Maybe this is the end of it."

"It's always good to be optimistic, but I have the feeling that this is only the very start of it," said Beatrice.

Posy returned to the shop to draft her email as Ramsay left to speak with Henrietta. Meadow and Beatrice remained, drinking coffee and mulling over the email.

Meadow said sternly, "I wish you hadn't said that you had a feeling this was only the start of some sort of trouble. We don't need any more trouble in Dappled Hills. This is an idyllic place. A quiet place! A safe place!"

"Most of the time," agreed Beatrice. "Until it's not."

Meadow said, "You know what I think this all is? It's jealousy."

"How do you figure that?" Beatrice reached down with resignation to pet Boris, who had laid his massive head on her leg.

"Because of who Henrietta is. That email was spiteful and I can't *think* of a reason that anyone would send it to shy little Henrietta unless it had to do with jealousy over her quilting ability. She does a very nice job with both machine quilting and piecing, and I think someone wishes *they* could quilt like that."

Boris looked adoringly into Beatrice's eyes as she scratched him behind the ears. She would have to thoroughly wash her hands before returning to Noo-noo or else her little corgi would be convinced she'd been cheating on her. "I'm not sure, Meadow. I don't know Henrietta like you do, but this doesn't sound like jealousy to me. I'm tending to agree with Ramsay—I think Henrietta may know something about someone."

Meadow waved her hand so energetically that coffee sloshed over the side and onto the table. "Who on earth does something like that, though? Let's say that Henrietta *does* know some sort of unsavory information about someone. Who on earth hacks into an email account and sends out a threatening email to everyone else?"

"Maybe someone who's afraid that Henrietta is going to spill their secret. You know how it is in a small town," said Beatrice. "No one wants everyone in their business all the time. Perhaps Henrietta is blackmailing someone and they've reached the point that they can't pay her anymore. Maybe she's threatening to tell everyone the secret."

Meadow shook her head. "It's just so hard to imagine. Let's talk about something else. I'm starting to feel like Ramsay—crime is overwhelming!"

"You're feeling like you need to escape to the back of the house with a copy of *The Importance of Being Earnest*?" asked Beatrice dryly. Ramsay, when he returned from talking with Henrietta, was almost certain to disappear with a favorite novel or book of poetry.

"Certainly not! But like I need to focus on something other than the dark side of people I know. Did you do your homework?" demanded Meadow.

"Oh!" said Beatrice. "Thanks for reminding me. The square is in my purse."

She pulled out a square framed in dark blue, with a yellow background. The words *Piper, will you marry me?* were centered in the middle and encircled by hearts, stars, and flowers.

"It looks beautiful," gasped Meadow. She teared up and even Beatrice found herself blinking hard.

Meadow added, "But that's not the homework I was talking about. Thanks for this, though ... I've made a huge amount of progress on the quilt."

"What? What homework...oh, you mean the phrase from Piper?" asked Beatrice.

"Her favorite poem or song or phrase," said Meadow. "Were you able to get it from her?"

"As a matter of fact," said Beatrice, "Piper suggested that I just use one word—*peace* or *love*."

Meadow gasped. "You didn't tell her what you were planning on doing with it, did you?"

"No, but I had to tell her *something* so that she wouldn't think that I was completely demented, Meadow. I told her that I was working on a quilt and was trying to experiment by incorporating words into it."

"Hmph. Well, okay. That's kind of basic, though. No favorite poem?" asked Meadow.

"She kept bringing up things like "The Lady of Shalott" and selections by Poe," said Beatrice. "I don't think that was going to do us any good."

"Well, shoot. Too bad that she had to have those sort of dire poems as favorites. I guess 'love' and/or 'peace' it will have to be. Now, moving on to some other things. How about the quilt show tomorrow? Are you all ready for it?" asked Meadow.

Beatrice sighed. Right now it seemed as though quilting were taking over her life. She had an exhibit in the quilt show to get ready, a mystery quilt, and the upcoming Sew and Tell. With all the activities, it was a wonder she had any time to work on the actual quilting. She said, "Well, the quilt for the show is done, at any rate."

"But the label? Have you sewn your label in with the date, name of the quilt, your name and contact info, and your techniques?" Meadow recited sternly.

"I haven't gotten that far," said Beatrice. "Maybe once I get home. I also need to roll the quilt for loose threads."

"Not only that, but you'll need a four-inch hanging sleeve for this show," said Meadow.

Beatrice groaned. "Somehow I forgot that. Do you think it has to be a matching fabric?"

Meadow's horrified expression answered that question.

"I can pick up some extra backing fabric at the Patchwork Cottage to match the quilt," said Beatrice, standing and giving Boris a goodbye pat. "And now I've really got to go if I've got all that to do."

"See you there tomorrow, if I don't see you before then," said Meadow cheerily. "And I'll show you the proposal quilt tomorrow!"

Beatrice sincerely hoped she wouldn't see Meadow before then. She had the feeling she'd be scurrying enough as it was.

Luckily, it ended up being a remarkably quiet afternoon and evening. She and Noo-noo even had time to take a quick, energetic walk after Beatrice had been sitting for a while and needed to move. Beatrice made herself a fast pasta meal, using jarred pasta sauce and found it surprisingly satisfying. Once she'd finished preparing her blazing stars quilt (a pattern she'd found challenging to complete), she went directly to bed.

The next day, Beatrice got a good deal accomplished. She took her quilt to the town hall for the quilt show set-up.

As she was about to leave, she saw Henrietta coming in, struggling with a couple of quilts. She wore a pair of black slacks and a simple black top with a pair of black patent-leather shoes. Beatrice held the door open for her and then hesitated. "Can I help you get set up?" she asked.

Henrietta smiled at her. It was something of a pinched smile, but Beatrice gathered that was common for Henrietta. "That would be great. It's Beatrice, isn't it?"

"And you're Henrietta," said Beatrice, taking one of the rolled-up quilts from Henrietta.

Henrietta gave her a rueful smile. "I'm afraid I'm easy to remember right now. I appear to be notorious."

Beatrice gave her a sympathetic look. "I got the email, so don't worry that I heard about it from any gossiping."

"That's cold comfort," said Henrietta, pressing her lips together grimly. "Oh, the joys of small town life."

Beatrice helped her gently unroll one of the quilts when they reached her display area. "Do you have any idea why someone would send an email like that?"

Henrietta bent to unroll another quilt and Beatrice could no longer see her face. "Pure spite?"

Beatrice started saying, "Spite over what—?" and then stopped as she took a look at the quilt she'd just unfurled. There must be over a hundred different fabrics hand-sewn into a quilt that looked almost like a painting. The result was something that Beatrice would have liked to display when she was a curator at the folk art museum. The quilt featured a peaceful scene of a sunset reflected in a lake as sailboats floated through. The sky was pieced with diamonds of various vividly colored fabrics. The effect was stunning.

"Oh, I see," said Beatrice quietly as she surveyed the quilt.

Henrietta stood again, giving her a wary look. She relaxed a bit at Beatrice's appraising and appreciative stare.

Beatrice said dryly, "I'm guessing you've won a lot of prizes. Have you got more like these?"

"Several. The rest are home." Henrietta hesitated. "Would you like to see them? Maybe after the show this evening, if you're not burned out on quilts by then."

Beatrice knew she was meeting Wyatt for supper, but figured popping over briefly wouldn't hurt. "That would be great. I used to be an art museum curator and I'd love to see more of your work."

They both turned at a voice from behind them. "Beatrice!" Hurrying toward them were sisters Savannah and Georgia, her friends from the Village Quilters guild. They gave Beatrice a quick hug and then smiled at Henrietta uncertainly. They'd have been on Posy's mystery quilt email list, too.

The sisters were completely different and it was amazing that they were as close as they were. Savannah's plain face was pointed and serious with a beaky nose and dark eyebrows that could potentially use some shaping. She carried herself with stiff comportment. Her sister, Georgia, was a much softer version of Savannah with pretty features, dancing eyes, and a rounded face with dimples.

Georgia was the first to recover and fill in the awkward silence. "Your quilts are absolutely *gorgeous*," she told Henrietta reverently. "I feel like I'm taking a vacation when I look at them."

Savannah, always a fan of geometrical patterns, squinted in an evaluating manner at the quilts before breaking out in a grin. "Amazing," she said gruffly.

If Savannah liked a non-geometrical quilt, it was truly outstanding.

Henrietta attempted to appear modest, although Beatrice saw that it was something of a struggle. But she clearly was aware of her talent and the ingenuity she applied to her craft. Henrietta said politely, "What have y'all brought to show today?"

"Nothing nearly as innovative, although I'm rather proud of my blazing stars quilt. It was a challenge that I struggled to meet, but it turned out better than I hoped," said Beatrice.

Savannah said, "I'd like to see it before you go, Beatrice. I brought in an Aztec design."

Beatrice knew that Savannah's quilt would be technically perfect, as always. She had quite the eye for detail.

"It sounds lovely," said Henrietta politely.

"And I'm not showing today—I'm just here to support all of you," said Georgia. "I've been so busy lately with school and with my pet clothes business that I haven't had enough time."

Savannah added slyly, "And busy with Tony."

Tony Brock worked at the hardware store in downtown Dappled Hills and was Georgia's boyfriend ... now her fiancé.

"Maybe just a little bit," said Georgia with a grin.

Beatrice said, "You and Tony must be getting excited about your wedding! What have you got planned so far?"

She hoped she didn't sound too nosy, but she felt as if she needed to do a little bit of recognizance in terms of how people actually *planned* weddings in Dappled Hills. Wyatt's sister, Harper, had gotten married there, but Beatrice had been more on the periphery in terms of helping plan the wedding. As the mother of the bride, Beatrice knew she would have to be a lot more on the ball this time.

Georgia said shyly, "Well, we're mainly just trying to see what's available in our budget. At first we thought we'd want something really small and intimate with just family and a few very close friends. But we had a hard time with that. How could I invite one person and not another ... in Dappled Hills? Tony and I feel like most of the town is almost like family. So we wanted to expand it to invite more of our friends. But we want it to be affordable, too. And fun! We have been so busy trying to figure out how to do that that we haven't even set our date yet. The only things we've planned for sure are that we want Wyatt to officiate at the ceremony and we want June Bug to be in charge of the cake. Savannah will still be my only attendant."

"There's June Bug, now," said Henrietta. "Just seeing her is making me think of cake."

The little woman with the round, flushed face was hurrying through the exhibit area. Hurrying was what June Bug did best. She used to keep a little *too* busy by cleaning houses and baking cakes for anyone who wanted one. Beatrice and Meadow had helped June Bug set up a cake shop and bakery in downtown Dappled Hills. She was probably just as busy, but at least usually in one place. Aside from today, of course. When she spotted them, she smiled and trotted over to talk. She'd become so much more animated and confident since starting her cake shop. Although she was still very quiet and shy, the shop seemed to help her become more outgoing. Maybe that's because she had so many customers to interact with—a testament to the success of the shop.

Georgia said, "You must have been asked to supply cake today for the quilt show."

"Now I'm *really* looking forward to the quilt show!" said Savannah.

"Just protect the cake from Miss Sissy," said Beatrice dryly. "Otherwise, it'll all disappear."

June Bug, familiar with Miss Sissy's appetite, looked alarmed. Or maybe she didn't—she had a perpetually startled expression to begin with. "Is Miss Sissy here now?"

"No, but I think Meadow is bringing her for the show," said Beatrice. "On the upside, she'll buy all the cake slices at the concessions stand." The women laughed and then Beatrice asked, "How are things going at June Bug's Cakes?"

June Bug's eyes glowed. "Oh, they're going really well. And I can't thank you enough, Beatrice."

Beatrice and Meadow had helped to physically set up the shop: moving chairs and tables in, adding pictures and quilts on the walls, and coming up with menus. But they'd also lent June Bug a little money to help her get started there. It was worth it to see the hardworking woman succeed.

"I'll be in there soon," promised Beatrice. "I can't wait to have more of those muffins. I still think that we should have called your store 'June Bug's Cakes and Bakery.'"

Savannah frowned in thought. "Not as catchy."

"No. But more descriptive."

Beatrice noticed that Henrietta's pleasant expression had faded and hardness was reflected in her eyes for a brief second before her face became impassive. Beatrice turned to see Orrilla Bush, one of the Cut-Ups that she'd been introduced to in the past, looking coldly in Henrietta's direction. Orrilla wore a dark suit that hung on her tall, thin frame. She had high cheekbones and artfully highlighted hair. Everything about her looked hard.

June Bug beamed at them all and said, "Better run!" before scurrying off.

Beatrice asked, "So any other plans for the wedding so far?"

Savannah said, "I'm still trying to get Smoke as the ring bearer. Wouldn't he be adorable in a little tuxedo?"

Georgia laughed. "He would steal the show, for sure. The only problem with that scenario is that Smoke does whatever Smoke wants to do. He's a cat, after all. He's just as likely to curl up on the aisle and take a nap as he is to prance down it with the ring."

As Georgia continued talking about the pros and cons of having a cat as a ring bearer, Henrietta murmured, "Excuse me," and walked over to stand in front of Orrilla.

Savannah said with more animation that she usually showed, "Smoke would be precious, I'm telling you! And wait until I tell you what he did this morning. He's the cleverest cat ever! Georgia designed several adorable bowties for him, and when I was putting them out, he actually nosed one to choose it!" She was always a little softer when she talked about her cat. The little gray cat had really worked his way into Savannah's heart.

Beatrice smiled and nodded but her glance kept flickering over to where Henrietta stood with Orrilla. She couldn't see Henrietta's face, but her stance seemed strangely relaxed. Orrilla's, on the other hand, was anything but. Orrilla stared intently at Henrietta, tautness in the hardness of her face. She reached out to grab Henrietta's arm as she made to turn away. For a moment, she gripped her arm tightly until finally shoving it and Henrietta away from her. Beatrice saw that the encounter left angry red marks on Henrietta's arm.

Chapter Four

Henrietta, remarkably calm, brushed her hand over the spot on her arm as if to remove a bit of dirt. Then she walked away toward the other side of the room. Orrilla had angry tears in her eyes as she stormed out of the building.

Beatrice realized that Savannah and Georgia appeared to be expecting some sort of a reply. She quickly said, "Well, of course! Smoke is the smartest, cutest cat ever."

The sisters beamed at her.

Beatrice added, "Sorry if I seem at all distracted. I was just watching a really odd interaction between Orrilla and Henrietta. Do you know Henrietta very well?"

They both shook their heads. Georgia said, "We used to see her a little more often than we do now. But a lot of the Cut-Ups have been too busy to go to shows and things."

"Looking at the detail in Henrietta's quilts, I can see why she's spending so much time at home," said Beatrice. "I almost feel as if I'm looking at a painting."

Savannah said, "That email that we got is worrying, though. Did Ramsay say anything about it? Henrietta doesn't seem like the sort of person to get talked about like that." Her stern features expressed rigid disapproval.

"Being called a liar like that was pretty bad," said Georgia with a shiver. "And of course she wouldn't know who it was from, so she'd be suspicious of everyone. Poor Posy for getting her email hacked like that."

Beatrice said thoughtfully, "Well, I don't think she'd be suspicious of *everyone*. So maybe it will be worth seeing who she does seem wary of. Clearly she wouldn't be worried about any of us. We don't have anything for anyone to gossip about, unless they're interested in Smoke's bowties or Georgia's hikes with Tony or my endlessly rescheduled dates with Wyatt."

"You think maybe Orrilla could have had something to do with it? Based on what you just saw?" asked Savannah with a frown. "What was this 'odd interaction'?"

"Maybe. They were definitely having an argument about something. But if so, then I'm surprised that Orrilla would engage in a scene with Henrietta and tip her off that she was involved. She even grabbed her arm hard to the point I was wondering if they were going to have a physical fight. I'm thinking there could be others," said Beatrice.

"Other whats?" asked a cheerful voice. "Quilts? Then you're in the right place."

Beatrice turned to see a plump woman wearing thick glasses. Her broad grin displayed crooked teeth and she had a cap of graying hair. Beatrice had the feeling that they'd met before, but she couldn't remember her name.

"Hi Hazel!" said Georgia. "Beatrice, have you met Hazel? She's a member of the Cut-Ups."

"I think we've met before. Good to see you, Hazel," said Beatrice. "Have you brought a quilt for the show?"

"An old one," said Hazel. "Haven't been able to motivate myself to work on anything new for a while. You know how it is—life gets busy. I have this adorable grandbaby in Charlotte that I've been trying to see every chance I get. That does take some time away from quilting."

Savannah said with a frown, "But didn't you tell me you were going to help Posy out?"

"With the Sew and Tell set-up? Of course. Although I don't have anything to really *show*!" said Hazel with a guffaw. "Maybe listening to everyone tell about their quilts will inspire me. I just wanted to help Posy out. She's always just so sweet. I could eat her up!"

"Savannah and I are helping out too, so we'll see you there. We were excited to hear about all the new events at the Patchwork Cottage," said Georgia.

Savannah said grimly, "Although I'm not real sure about the mystery quilt."

Georgia gave her sister a fond smile. "I thought you'd gotten over that. We talked about how it's important to try new things. It's really the only way to grow."

Beatrice hid a smile. Savannah's obsession with geometric prints was obviously spilling over with her worries about the mystery quilt. "I'm sure Posy wouldn't come up with anything too radical. Besides, it's supposed to be fun."

Hazel said, eyes open wide, "*Supposed* to be fun is right. What on earth was that weird email all about? Oh, I know Posy didn't have anything to do with it, but who did? And why?"

Savannah's voice was brusque. "Obviously nothing to do with Henrietta. Just someone being mean and playing around with a computer. Case closed."

Hazel's face fell comically. Beatrice could tell she'd been looking forward to either a gossip session or was being nosy and hoping for some information.

"You don't think where there's smoke, there's fire?" asked Hazel a bit pitifully.

Savannah put her hands on her thin hips. "There was no smoke. There was just a bully."

Hazel's shoulders slumped a little. Then she brightened a bit as she spotted local cake shop owner June Bug rushing in with a tray of cakes. "Oh good. At least we know there'll be good food later."

And there was. Everyone was buying slices of June Bug's delicious cakes and there were also some tasty pimento cheese finger sandwiches and sweet tea.

Beatrice's neighbor and fellow-quilter, Miss Sissy, texted Beatrice and asked for a ride to the quilt show. She apparently wasn't showing anything this time since she hadn't been there at the show set-up and didn't have a quilt with her now. The old woman galloped out the door, her wiry gray hair slipping wildly out of the knot at the top of her head. She was in quite an aloof mood and sat in stony silence on the short ride to the quilt show. Until, of course, she'd gotten out of the car in a huff, hissing, "Crazy driver!" and shaking a thin fist in Beatrice's direction. Considering Miss Sissy was something of an aficionado of sidewalk driving, Beatrice decided to ignore the complaint.

There were many different types of quilts and quilting at the show and plenty for Beatrice to both feast her eyes on and want to find out more about. The show had provided categories for the different styles and techniques in an attempt to judge apples to apples. The categories included everything from appliqué, to piecing, to use of negative space. Although there were definitely some unique quilts there, nothing caught Beatrice's eye as much as Henrietta's quilt.

Meadow was busy making a determined effort to persuade everyone she saw to take part in Posy's Sew and Tell and mystery quilt. That was all well and good for the mystery quilt, since it was mostly an emailed event, but Beatrice decided if Meadow drummed up any more support for the Sew and Tell that Posy's shop would be bursting at the seams.

Meadow came over to talk to Beatrice toward the end of the event. "Where's Henrietta?" asked Beatrice, glancing around. "They're about to announce the judges' decisions and I'm sure she's about to receive a ribbon for her quilts."

"Oh, she had a headache," said Meadow. "She left early."

Beatrice wondered if the other quilters hadn't been the cause of her headache. Orrilla, in particular. Every time she'd seen Orrilla during the show, she'd been glowering in Henrietta's direction.

Beatrice frowned. "I'm sorry to hear that, especially since I was supposed to run by her house after the show. She was going to briefly show me some of her other quilts."

"Why not text her and ask if it's okay if you still drop by? She probably was just ready to leave the crowd here and is looking forward to showing you her quilts. Wouldn't you? It's not every day an art museum curator wants to review your stuff, you know."

"Retired curator," said Beatrice. "And I don't have her number."

Meadow pulled out her phone. "I'll send you the contact number. No excuses!"

Beatrice jumped as Miss Sissy's wizened face abruptly appeared at her shoulder. "Miss Sissy! I didn't realize you were there."

"I want to go," said the old woman, a mulish expression on her face.

Beatrice's phone beeped as Meadow's text message came through. She typed a message to Henrietta as Meadow said in a placating voice, "Now, Miss Sissy. How about I take you home instead of Beatrice?"

"I want to see the quilts," said Miss Sissy, a determined glint in her eye.

Meadow said, "But you can't let Beatrice hog you, Miss Sissy! I haven't been able to get a visit with you for ages."

Miss Sissy just stared at her with her hard, black button eyes.

Beatrice sighed. "Okay, Miss Sissy. You can come along with me. I just got a reply from Henrietta and she says it's fine for me to run by. But I'm not staying for very long, okay?"

Meadow asked with lively curiosity on her face, "The long-awaited date with Wyatt?"

"That's right. Finally. We've been trying to schedule this for a while, but it's been tough between his schedule and mine," said Beatrice. "How is everything going with the—well, you know."

She had a feeling Miss Sissy wasn't wonderful about keeping secrets.

Unfortunately, this only served to pique the old woman's interest. Her eyes narrowed as her focus shifted to Meadow. There was a brief interlude where the judges' decisions were announced, revealing that Henrietta had indeed won a ribbon. The interlude did nothing to distract Miss Sissy.

Meadow turned pink. This may have been due to the fact that Meadow was also bad at keeping secrets, especially when someone clearly wanted to know the secret. But if she let something slip to Miss Sissy, Piper would hear about the engagement before it even happened.

"Um," Meadow looked helplessly at Beatrice.

Beatrice quickly added, "That is to say, how is your ... experimental ... quilt going, Meadow? Progressing?"

"Done, actually," said Meadow. "Except for just finishing up."

Upon closer inspection, Meadow did have circles under her eyes. It must have been a long night.

"It looks beautiful," said Meadow with a happy sigh. "But I'll admit that I'm ready to go home and turn in. Although I don't feel like cooking. Maybe I can get the 'early bird special' at the diner like the rest of the seniors in Dappled Hills. Supper at four-thirty p.m., turning in at six-thirty. I feel old. At least they're displaying our quilts for a week so we don't have to take everything down tonight."

"Even a teenager would feel old if she stayed up all night," said Beatrice. "In fact, I'm exhausted, myself, and I've got a full evening ahead. Miss Sissy, is it all right if we go ahead and head out? I'll get Henrietta's ribbon from the judges and give it to her while we're there."

Miss Sissy grunted in agreement and they headed out for a short drive to Henrietta's house. They parked in the short driveway of a small ranch-style house with carefully pruned shrubs and beds of colorful marigolds and daylilies.

"Now, like I said, only a few minutes, Miss Sissy," warned Beatrice. She felt as if she were giving a small child the five-minute warning before leaving a playground. "Wyatt and I have dinner plans and I still need to go home and get ready."

"Tell Wyatt hi," said the old woman gruffly. She always had a warm spot for Wyatt, who dropped by to visit her weekly and always had a small treat in hand when he did.

Beatrice shifted the blue ribbon to her other hand and knocked firmly at the faded, red front door and waited for a few seconds, listening for footsteps or other sounds. Hearing nothing, she frowned.

Miss Sissy pointed a crooked, arthritic finger. "Doorbell," she said.

"I know, but I always feel doorbells are so startling and intrusive that I almost hate disturbing the peace with them," said Beatrice. But by the time she was finished with her short speech on doorbells, Miss Sissy had already pushed the button several times with great determination.

Miss Sissy shrugged a thin shoulder. "She knew we were coming."

"Knew *I* was coming," said Beatrice. She frowned again. "That's kind of odd. Maybe she's in her laundry room or is taking a shower or something."

Beatrice knocked once more, a resounding knock and Miss Sissy reached out to press the doorbell another few times. No response.

"I think we should try to go in," said Beatrice. "Meadow said she was taken ill at the quilt show. Maybe she was worse off than anyone knew."

Miss Sissy was already turning the doorknob. The door opened and they walked in together. There were no lights on and the late-afternoon sunshine wasn't casting much illumination into Henrietta's house.

"Henrietta?" called Beatrice in a loud voice. "It's Beatrice and Miss Sissy. We wanted to see your quilts?"

The small house appeared empty. But they'd seen Henrietta's old sedan parked in the driveway. Beatrice could tell that Henrietta had talent with interior design, even if it appeared that she didn't have much cash to fund it. The walls were painted with a technique that provided texture to the walls and were in warm colors that complemented the fabrics she'd chosen for chairs and her sofa. Wood had been painted white and distressed for even more texture and to provide the overall country look that Henrietta seemed to have been aiming for.

When they walked into the living room, having looked through the rest of the house, Beatrice didn't see anything at first. No one was sitting on the sofa or at the rather cluttered computer desk.

As she was turning, Miss Sissy grabbed her forearm with surprising strength. "Look!" she said urgently.

That's when she saw a pair of patent-leather shoes sticking awkwardly out from the base of the sofa.

Chapter Five

Beatrice's breath caught in her throat. Miss Sissy was quickly backing up, spooked. Beatrice forced herself to be calm. "Miss Sissy," she said, a peremptory note in her voice, "would you call for help? You've got your phone?"

Miss Sissy nodded and seemed happy for the distraction as Beatrice quickly strode to the other side of the sofa. She stopped. Henrietta lay on the floor, a heavy sewing machine on top of her head. It had apparently fallen from the sofa table next to her.

Beatrice picked up Henrietta's wrist with shaking hands.

Miss Sissy was saying, "Calling Ramsay. No ambulance. Dead woman."

Miss Sissy was right. Henrietta was a dead woman. Beatrice gently laid down Henrietta's arm and stood up as Miss Sissy dialed Ramsay's number. She couldn't see any way this could be an accident. Henrietta was facing away from the table. It wasn't as if she'd stumbled, grabbed the table for support, and pulled the machine on top of herself. Even if that *had* been possible, the table would have fallen over as well. It looked like someone had deliberately and coldly pushed the sewing machine onto Henrietta.

Beatrice could tell that Ramsay was asking questions and that Miss Sissy didn't seem to be communicating effectively with him. When Beatrice reached out a hand, Miss Sissy handed the phone wordlessly over to her.

"Ramsay?" asked Beatrice. "Yes, I'm here, too. It's Henrietta Hunnicutt. I was invited to run by her house to see some of her quilts and Miss Sissy and I found her dead when we got here."

"I'm on my way," said Ramsay grimly.

Miss Sissy backed up until she was standing near the door. "Are you okay?" Beatrice asked. Miss Sissy gave a fierce nod and Beatrice said, "Good. I'm just going to glance around a second and see if I can figure out who's behind this."

"Don't touch!" said the old woman.

"I wouldn't dream of it," said Beatrice. "Or, at least, I'll touch only one thing." She laid the ribbon carefully on a nearby table without touching the table.

The only thing that really drew her attention in the room was the cluttered desk. The rest of the living room and, in fact, the rest of the small house, was immaculately tidy.

She walked over to the desk and peered at the papers covering the top of it. Then Beatrice stooped to peer closer. There was a list of names—names of quilters on one piece of paper. Beside each name there was a dollar amount that varied widely. Beatrice saw Julia Tharpe's name with one hundred dollars next to it. Then she spotted Hazel Struby's name with forty dollars beside it. Were these quilting-related guild fees of some kind? Or something else?

Beatrice reached in her purse to pull out her phone, remembering that taking a picture could be useful. But the battery was dead. "Miss Sissy, I don't remember. Does your phone take pictures?"

Miss Sissy said scornfully. "No. It's for talking and texting on."

Beatrice pulled out a small notebook from her purse and a pencil. She noted the names she saw with the dollar amounts: Minerva Lundy, Orrilla Bush, Hazel Struby, and Julia Tharpe. Her pencil hovered over her notebook as she saw another scrap of paper with more writing on it. This one looked more like doodles of the sort one might make while talking on the phone. There was a sketch showing a thin woman with dark hair and eyes. When Beatrice noticed the pearl earrings and pearl necklace on the woman on the sketch, she realized it was a picture of Julia Tharpe. She also realized that Henrietta had drawn daggers pointed right at Julia and put an X over her face. That didn't seem like the friendliest of drawings.

The door had been unlocked and Beatrice hadn't noticed any broken windows or other signs of a break-in. Keeping the threatening email in mind, it certainly looked as if Henrietta had been murdered by someone she knew. She'd let whomever in the house, lost her balance or perhaps been pushed or shoved, and then the killer had knocked the heavy sewing machine on top of her. Then the killer had walked back out the door.

Miss Sissy remained absorbed in her focused study of the quilt. Beatrice heard a car drive up outside and hurried footsteps. "It's okay, Miss Sissy," she said quietly, "Ramsay's here."

Judging from the fresh spill on his shirt, Ramsay appeared to have been eating supper when he got the call. He said urgently, "Are you both okay?" Getting a nod from both Miss Sissy and Beatrice, he added as he started striding toward the feet he saw around the side of the sofa, "No sign of any intruder when you arrived?"

"Nothing," said Beatrice simply. "And we were sure not to touch anything. I just laid Henrietta's blue ribbon from the quilt show down."

"Do you ladies mind waiting for me by my car?" asked Ramsay. "Just in case there's any evidence of any kind that I need to protect."

Miss Sissy, still clearly disturbed by the events, was already halfway out the door when Beatrice turned to follow.

They waited for what seemed a long time before Ramsay appeared again. He was rubbing the side of his face with his hand and apparently had been doing so for quite a while, judging from the red mark on his face.

Finally he said to them, "The state police are on their way with a forensic team. Although, to me, it all looks fairly cut and dried." He gave Beatrice a questioning look as if wanting to see if she agreed with him.

Beatrice cleared her throat. "Especially keeping the email in mind."

"Wickedness!" hissed Miss Sissy. She appeared on the verge of being extremely worked up and was worrying a button on her long dress to the point that Beatrice wondered if it would pop off.

Ramsay gave the old woman a wary look. "Now, now. Everything is fine, Miss Sissy. We'll work through this. Here, why don't you take a seat in my police car while we wait? It may be that the state police would like to talk to you both, although I'm also going to take a statement from you."

Miss Sissy, still muttering under her breath, stomped off to sit in the back of the police cruiser.

Beatrice said, "It must have been murder. There's no way that I can think of that Henrietta's death was an accident."

"Especially considering that email," said Ramsay. "As you said. Which leads me to my next question. I know that from time to time there's gossip going on in the quilting community."

Beatrice hid a smile. Ramsay spoke as if it were fairly unusual for the quilters to talk about each other.

"And I know if I were to ask Meadow, she'd say that everything was hunky-dory with the quilters. She'd insist that Henrietta Hunnicutt was the nicest woman she'd ever known. She was even trying to convince me that a hacker from outside Dappled Hills had hacked Posy's email to threaten Henrietta since there was *no way* that anyone in our community would do such a thing." Ramsay shook his head at the type of issues that he had to deal with.

"A hacker from outside Dappled Hills. Who knew Henrietta's name." Beatrice's voice was dry.

"Meadow was sure it was a Russian hacker intent on evildoing," said Ramsay with a hint of a smile.

Beatrice said, "I'm pretty sure that it was a quilter that Henrietta knew. She apparently isn't winning any popularity contests with the Cut-Ups guild. Well, that might be overstating it. I can't speak for the entire guild, but I certainly noticed that Orrilla Bush was unhappy with Henrietta at the quilt show earlier."

"Orrilla Bush," mused Ramsay. "Somehow I can't see Orrilla getting into fisticuffs at a quilt show."

"A very reserved woman, ordinarily," agreed Beatrice. "And it definitely wasn't a physical altercation, although Orrilla did grip Henrietta's arm quite fiercely at one point. It was more of a furious confrontation. But Orrilla seems too smart to send a threatening email and then get into a public argument with someone she's about to murder."

"Getting back to the murder," said Ramsay. "Let me get this straight. I know I *should* see how this all fits into quilting, but I can't keep all of Meadow's quilting events straight. Can you just briefly hit the highlights of the timeline here?" He absently patted his pockets before pulling out a small notepad and pencil from his right pocket.

"The threatening email you know about—that was days ago," said Beatrice. "By the way, you said you were going to ask Henrietta about it. Did she give any insights?"

"None," said Ramsay succinctly. "She simply thought it was a childish prank by someone jealous of her quilting ability."

Which was very similar to what Henrietta had told Beatrice. "Hmm," she said.

Ramsay lifted an eyebrow. "I'm taking it that she probably knew more than that and didn't want to let on?"

"That's what I'm thinking. Generally, there's not the kind of jealousy in the quilting community over ability that would prompt someone to send out a nasty email like that. I wondered if maybe Henrietta wasn't as nice as Meadow would like to believe," said Beatrice.

Ramsay nodded. "Okay. So the nasty email goes out and Henrietta sort of pooh-poohs the whole thing. Then you have the quilt show today and you witness some sort of quarrel between Henrietta and Orrilla Bush. That likely *wasn't* over Henrietta's quilting aptitude."

"Yes. Except what I witnessed was at the quilt show set-up. That was earlier today."

Ramsay made a note. "And then you left and returned later for the quilt show. Henrietta wasn't there, though?"

"She *was* there, but she wasn't there for the whole show. She told Meadow that she had a headache and left early. I asked her if it were still all right for me to come by and see some of her other quilts. During the set-up, she'd noticed how interested I was in her quilting, knew my background as a curator, and invited me to drop by briefly."

Ramsay looked sharply after her. "So you were likely the last one to speak to her."

"Besides whoever killed her," said Beatrice, a sad note in her voice. "I know it's likely that she was mixed up in something that led to her death, but she was friendly to me and did create some beautiful art through her quilting."

"What time do you think it was when you talked to her?" asked Ramsay.

Beatrice said thoughtfully, "I didn't actually *talk* to her at all. Meadow texted me Henrietta's phone number, but I texted instead of calling her. It just seemed less-intrusive, especially if she wasn't feeling well."

Beatrice and Ramsay looked at each other. "So what you're telling me," said Ramsay, "is that potentially, the killer could have been the one who texted you back."

"That's right. Although I can't think of a reason the murderer would do such a thing." But Beatrice stopped, because suddenly she could definitely think of a reason. What if the killer had returned to the quilt show in time for the awards? The text message would make it look as if Henrietta had possibly been murdered after she had been—giving the killer enough time to establish an alibi.

Ramsay made a note. "I think you've already come up with a reason for that to happen. And I'm not saying you *didn't* get a text from Henrietta herself, but we just can't be sure. Let's move onto the quilt show and who was there and when."

Beatrice shook her head. "There were a good number of people there. And some of the people I noticed were from the set-up time—like Orrilla. Hazel Struby was also there at set-up. And, of course, during the show, they don't stay in one spot where you can see them. The room is set up to hang quilts, so there are lots of screens up. It's probably the perfect way to leave and then return without being seen. I didn't even notice that Henrietta had left until it was nearly time for the awards and I didn't see her there."

Ramsay said, "Let's start with her own quilt guild. Just who you *saw* at some point there. I'll ask others the same thing and maybe I can piece it together. Because, considering that email, I'm thinking it's someone she knew from quilting."

Beatrice added slowly, "And someone who knew that she *was* at home. Someone who might have seen her leave the quilt show. Unfortunately, I've realized that I don't know all the Cut-Ups as well as I should." She glanced over at Ramsay's police car. Miss Sissy sat sedately in the backseat. A car drove past and she shook her fist at it. "Let's ask Miss Sissy. She knows *all* the quilters."

"Yes, but does she know their names? And how accurate is her memory? Does she even want to cooperate?" asked Ramsay dryly.

Miss Sissy still seemed on edge from her frightening discovery in the house. She gave Ramsay and Beatrice a wary look as they approached, but stepped reluctantly out and away from the police car to speak to them. Miss Sissy had the tendency to be extremely curious.

Ramsay said in a kind voice, "We were trying to figure out who might have been at the quilt show this afternoon, Miss Sissy."

Her eyes narrowed. "Why?"

"Well, it might help us find out who could behind Henrietta's death," said Beatrice.

Miss Sissy deflated a bit, slumping at the mention of Henrietta. "Wickedness," she muttered.

"Exactly," said Ramsay, without missing a beat.

"Fighting!" hissed Miss Sissy.

"Who was fighting?" asked Ramsay intently. "Someone was arguing with Henrietta?"

"No!" said Miss Sissy scornfully. "*Henrietta* fighting with someone."

Beatrice took a deep breath meant to help give her more patience. "Who was the quilter that Henrietta was arguing with?"

"That one with the blonde hair!" said Miss Sissy, flashing her a resentful look for pushing the subject.

Ramsay nodded. "Okay." He turned to look at Beatrice. "Ring any bells?"

"Not *really*. There are several quilters who've sort of frosted their hair and it may have looked blonde. Oh, wait." Beatrice turned to Miss Sissy. "Do you mean the woman who has that dyed-blonde bang? The rest of her hair is a different color—more of a chestnut."

Miss Sissy nodded.

"Well, at least it's something to start out with. She's in the Cut-Ups, right?" asked Ramsay.

Miss Sissy said, "Cut-Ups. The blonde. Arguing!" The old woman sounded most indignant at the fact that there was unrest at the quilt show.

"Okay, okay, got it," said Ramsay soothingly. "Who else do you remember being there—especially if they had a run-in with Henrietta?"

But Miss Sissy appeared to be tapped out. She gave a shrug of her bony shoulder and galloped off for the backseat of the police car.

Ramsay glanced at the road at the sound of approaching cars. "That'll be the state police. At least I'm getting somewhere ... I think."

Beatrice said hesitantly, "You know, while Miss Sissy and I were waiting for you, I noticed there was a list inside. It looked to be members of the Cut-Ups."

Ramsay nodded, watching as the cars pulled up to the curb in front of Henrietta's house. "I saw it. Figured it had to do with some sort of quilt project or something." He looked closer at Beatrice. "You think it might not?"

"I don't know. I guess it *could*. But the amounts were all different and there was some sort of mean-spirited doodling on there, too. Combined with the email everyone got about Henrietta being a liar, I wondered if maybe she wasn't trying to blackmail people she knew. I know she was doing some interior design work—maybe her fellow guild members had tried to give her some business and she'd found information on them during her time in their homes."

Ramsay made a note in his notebook. "Well, if she was blackmailing people, we'll soon find out. That's the kind of thing that will stand out in her checking account—small, regular deposits over a period of time. And now I'd better go. You'll stick around for the state police to shoot a question or two at you?"

It really wasn't a question. Beatrice decided she might as well join Miss Sissy in the police car to wait. When she climbed in, she saw that Miss Sissy was fast asleep and snoring with gusto.

The sun was going down when Ramsay finally gestured to Beatrice to speak to one of the state police investigators. She was about to step out of the car when she froze. Wyatt. She'd completely, if somewhat understandably, forgotten about Wyatt. And, of course, her phone was completely dead.

"Miss Sissy?"

The old woman continued snoring with abandon.

Beatrice reached over to tentatively touch Miss Sissy's arm.

Miss Sissy jumped, reared back, and stared suspiciously at Beatrice.

"I'm sorry to wake you. But could I borrow your phone? Wyatt has no idea where I am and we were supposed to go out together," said Beatrice.

Miss Sissy patted the pocket of her loosely fitting dress and pulled out the flip phone, handing it to her. "Need it back," she growled.

"In just a second," promised Beatrice. She started texting awkwardly on the phone, stopping for a moment to call to Ramsay, "I'm sorry. I'll just be a minute."

She wrote: *Wyatt, this is Beatrice on Miss Sissy's phone.*

A text message from Wyatt came back. *Everything okay?*

Beatrice rubbed her forehead with her free hand. The fact she'd forgotten about their dinner, made her flush.

So sorry! Ugh. Something urgent came up. Miss Sissy and I are fine. You at the restaurant? For the life of her, she couldn't remember if she and Wyatt had planned on meeting at the restaurant or if he were picking her up first.

No—outside your house. It's okay, now that I know you're all right. Noo-noo keeping an eye on me through the curtains. Should I keep waiting?

Beatrice typed quickly back: *No, afraid need to resched. So sorry.*

Ramsay introduced her to a Lieutenant Thomas with the SBI (State Bureau of Investigation) for North Carolina. He had a trim physique, short hair, and tired eyes. But she learned that he was certainly thorough in terms of asking questions. When

Beatrice finally finished speaking with Lieutenant Thomas, it was completely dark out. What's more, she felt absolutely exhausted from the discovery.

Ramsay asked, "Do you mind taking Miss Sissy home? I think I'm going to be a while or else I'd take her myself. And Beatrice—be sure to get some sleep. You're looking pretty worn out."

Ramsay didn't have to tell her twice. She took Miss Sissy back (the old woman muttered to herself the entire time about death and bodies and evil, which didn't make for a light atmosphere), took Noo-noo out as soon as she got home, and crawled right into bed.

Chapter Six

Saturday morning, Beatrice called Wyatt first thing after breakfast. "I'm sure you've probably already heard about Henrietta's death," she started out.

He gently interrupted her. "I sure have, Beatrice, and I'm very sorry about it. I'm also very worried about you and Miss Sissy. That must have been awful for both of you."

"It was, actually. Absolutely awful. I think it's because we were in her home and sort of creeping through and it all felt so eerie. And then, when Miss Sissy spotted Henrietta, it was just this horrid sensation in the pit of my stomach. She had made these extraordinary quilts and had invited me to drop by and see some others, since I was so interested. It's all just such a shame." Beatrice sighed. "I was just going to briefly drop by before taking Miss Sissy home and then enjoy a nice dinner with you. I'm sorry that our plans fell through. And in such a tragic way."

"Don't think a thing about it. Just take care of yourself today, Beatrice. Get some extra rest. Read a book. Do something you enjoy doing to get your mind off it. We'll set up another date for a dinner soon."

His kind words made Beatrice get a lump in her throat, as kindness always somehow seemed to do. "Thanks, Wyatt."

She'd no sooner hung up with Wyatt then there was a knock at her front door. She peered out and saw Meadow and Ash standing there, both looking concerned. Ash towered over Meadow and the frown on his handsome features turned into a crooked grin of greeting when he saw Beatrice standing there.

When Beatrice opened the door, Meadow flung herself at her for a hug. "When I think how close you might have come to the killer! It doesn't bear thinking about."

Ash reached out for a hug as soon as Meadow had given up her spot. "We're so glad you're all right, Beatrice."

"Ramsay told me all about it last night. Absolutely horrible. I'd have been over here last night to make sure you were all right, but he *assured* me that you were fine."

Fortunately, Meadow was more distracted than usual because she'd finished the proposal quilt with the 'peace' and 'love' words incorporated.

Meadow beamed as she held up the quilt. It was a beautiful combination of Piper's favorite colors, 'peace' and 'love,' a photo of Piper and Ash together and smiling happily at the camera, and at the bottom right of the quilt, the machine embroidered message: *Piper, will you marry me?* The yellow and light blue lent a cheerful, hopeful tone.

"It's beautiful," said Beatrice, reaching out a hand to feel the smooth texture of the cloth. "And it's beautiful because of what it will mean for you and Piper." She hesitated and then added to Ash, "You've found such a thoughtful way to ask Piper to be your wife. I know you and she will be so happy together."

Ash said earnestly, choking up slightly by the end, "I can't thank you both enough. This quilt is such a beautiful way to ask Piper to share her life with me."

Seeing Ash get choked up got to both Meadow and Beatrice and soon they were hugging each other and Beatrice was hurrying off to find a box of tissues.

Meadow blew her nose emphatically and asked, "So Ash. *When*? When are you going to ask her?"

Beatrice shifted a bit uncomfortably, still feeling as if she was intruding a little on a private event.

Ash smiled at his mother. "Mom, you're going to have to wait until next weekend. I want to cook for Piper for her birthday and put the quilt in a gift bag for her as her present."

This promptly made Meadow burst into tears again. Beatrice shoved the box of tissues her way as Noo-noo looked at them all with concern.

"That's just so sweet," sobbed Meadow. "And I can't wait until we're all a family. I already *do* feel like we're family, and this will make it even more so. But how am I going to wait until this weekend?"

Beatrice said, "We have lots to do, remember? Posy just emailed out the next bit of instructions for the mystery quilt and the Sew and Tell is on Friday." She avoided mentioning the fact that she might want to talk to a few of the Cut-Ups to see if she could get information about Henrietta's death. Just so that Ash didn't think his future mother-in-law was actively pursuing detective work.

Meadow, however, had no such qualms. "Shouldn't we try to help Ramsay, too? No one wants to tell Ramsay the truth—it's quite annoying. And the state police don't seem to be getting anywhere, either. Although I like that nice Lieutenant Thomas from the SBI. Ramsay has brought him by the house and he said very complimentary things about my meat loaf."

"This is about the murder of your quilting friend?" Ash looked confused at the seeming non-sequitur.

"It certainly is. Beatrice, in particular, is excellent at getting people to talk about things they'd rather not talk about. It's a gift, really, and gifts should be used! We'll try to work in some casual questioning and help poor Ramsay out," said Meadow. "I don't think he wants to be shown up by Lieutenant Thomas. And besides, he despises police work and doesn't seem to mind Beatrice's help. Beatrice can start talking to everybody and get some answers!"

"And we'll be very careful when doing so," said Beatrice with a reassuring smile at Ash. "And only when we find very natural ways of asking very nosy questions."

Meadow said, "I guess we're going to be focusing on quilters?" She made a face.

"I don't see a way around it," said Beatrice. "Most of the people who'd have known about the mystery quilt and Posy's emails would have been quilters, unless they were a friend or family member of a quilter who spoke about them. And most of the people who would have seen the password to the email account at the checkout counter would have been quilters, unless they were accompanying a quilter to the shop. It's not *definitely* a quilter, but it's *most likely* a quilter."

Meadow sighed. "I had a feeling you were going to say that. Well, we *know* it's not one of the Village Quilters. Some of us barely know Henrietta, or just know her strictly from quilt shows."

Ash raised his eyebrows. "So one of the Cut-Ups is a killer?"

"As unlikely as that seems," said Meadow darkly.

Beatrice said, "We'll focus on them, yes. In fact, I think we'll start with the list of names I spotted on Henrietta's desk and maybe go from there. There's obviously something we don't know about. Maybe the reason that the Cut-Ups haven't been involved as much in the community lately is because they haven't been getting along."

Meadow snapped her fingers. "That makes sense! Maybe there's been some bad blood between them somehow and they've been trying to avoid each other by not shopping at the Patchwork Cottage and by dropping all their quilt shows and other events."

"At least you made some progress by reaching out to the Cut-Ups, right? The last I heard, you'd persuaded many of them to participate in the mystery quilt and the Sew and Tell," said Beatrice.

"Mom can be *very* persuasive," said Ash, a twinkle in his bright blue eyes.

"Don't I know it! That's how I ended up quilting in the first place," said Beatrice, grinning back at him.

"And it's a good thing I am, too! Now we'll have a chance to pry into the Cut-Ups business because they'll be out buying fabric and supplies and being part of our event, said Meadow. She frowned. "Although everyone will be holed up quilting for the next week," said Meadow, "To make some progress with their Sew and Tell quilt. It wouldn't do to show up with a pile of fabric and a pattern, would it? No, one would want to show *progress.*"

Beatrice sighed at the pile of fabric and pattern still in a bag over in the corner of the room.

As it happened, there *were* no opportunities to casually ask nosy questions. Meadow was right—the ladies were all holed up and working on their quilts. Or, rather, they were all holed up ... Beatrice wasn't exactly sure why. Ordinarily, they'd be scurrying around baking casseroles to bring to the bereaved family members of the friend who passed away. In this case, however, the bereaved was an elderly sister who lived on the other side of the country. The sister was, by all accounts, remotely making arrangements for the service and would be flying in the day before. In this particular instance, casseroles didn't seem to be called for, since the bereaved could hardly fly back with them.

Beatrice had nothing to do except her normal chores around the house, yard work, cooking, and quilting. She'd tried to reschedule her dinner with Wyatt, but he regretfully told her that he had to leave town for a conference. A minister from a neighboring town would apparently be helping with Henrietta's funeral in Wyatt's absence.

"How about Friday? That's when I come back to town," said Wyatt.

Beatrice hesitated. That was the day of the Sew and Tell. There really *shouldn't* be a conflict between the quilting event and dinner with Wyatt, but she'd hate to have to postpone dinner again if anything did create a conflict.

"Let's play it safe and shoot for Saturday," said Beatrice. "You'll probably be tired after your conference anyway, won't you? Or are you someone who gets *more* energized when you're in a group of people?"

"Oh no, I'll be tired," said Wyatt with a laugh. "You're right. Let's plan for Saturday. Would a picnic that day be all right? Something different?"

"Sounds lovely," said Beatrice. She crossed her fingers that the weather wouldn't create another reason for postponing their date.

It was Wednesday when Piper called her. "Just wanted to say hi," she said. "How's everything going there? How's your new project?"

"Which one?" asked Beatrice wryly. "The mystery quilt or the project for the Sew and Tell?"

"The one for the Sew and Tell. Are you liking it better than you thought you would?" asked Piper.

"Hmm?" Beatrice had the distinct impression that she was forgetting something important.

"You know. Integrating words on the quilt—you were asking me about my favorite lines of poetry?"

"Ohhh. Oh, yes. Well, you were very helpful with advice for that. Yes. And you were right that I should only tackle a word or two instead of trying too much the first time. And you reminded me that I hadn't *really* liked that type of quilt—for myself, that is," said Beatrice hurriedly.

"Did I scare you off?" asked Piper.

"Just made me rethink it, that's all. After all, why would I want to try something I've never worked on before when life is so busy?" asked Beatrice.

"Exactly why I think you need to make time for something relaxing and fun. Especially after the scare you and Miss Sissy had last week. Maybe plan something fun with Wyatt?" asked Piper.

This seemed like a good time to try and clear up Piper's calendar for Ash. "Already planned something. Speaking of making plans, I hope you've made some time with Ash for your birthday this weekend," said Beatrice.

"You know, I'm so slammed this weekend with grading papers and getting things ready for that school fundraiser. I was thinking that I would just postpone any celebrating for a while."

Uh-oh. This did not fit into Ash's master plan.

"Why don't you just leave a little time free? Maybe on Sunday evening? That way the papers wouldn't be hanging over your head, and you could get a chance to unwind for your birthday," said Beatrice.

Piper laughed and said, "Thanks for looking out for me. But I don't think I'll be in the mood to go out. Maybe I'll just treat myself to a frozen pizza and relax in my favorite old pjs."

This was probably not the romantic scene that Ash was envisioning, but at least Piper had agreed to set some time aside. Beatrice said her goodbyes, feeling she'd tried to do her part.

Thursday was Henrietta's funeral. As was so often the case for Southern funerals, it was a blazingly sunny day and relentlessly cheerful. Beatrice arrived twenty minutes before the service was to start and stood outside the funeral home tent.

Meadow had been tasked with bringing Miss Sissy, who seemed to be in better mental condition than Beatrice had seen her in lately. She was merely glowering at everyone, and was at least keeping quiet and not making any dire statements. Miss Sissy bobbed her head in greeting when she saw Beatrice before wandering off to talk to Ramsay.

Beatrice said to Meadow, "At least Miss Sissy seems to be in a good mood."

Meadow sighed. "You weren't there when I was telling her that she shouldn't wear a white linen sundress to a funeral."

"A white linen sundress? Where on earth did she dig that up? I haven't ever seen her in such a thing. Usually she's wearing perfectly appropriate long-sleeved dresses that go down to mid-calf or almost her ankle."

"Apparently she found it at the Goodwill store and was determined to show it off," said Meadow. "It was quite a struggle. I think she might have been just a wee bit distracting if she'd worn it." Her gaze scanned the funeral-goers. "So, who's our likely victim today?"

"Excuse me?" asked Beatrice, although she knew perfectly well what Meadow was referring to.

"You know! Who are we questioning today? You know as well as I do that a funeral is the perfect place to talk to suspects, or at least to watch them and their reactions. It's why Ramsay is here, for heaven's sake. Do you think I could have gotten Ramsay Downey to a funeral on a beautiful day if the poor woman had perished from cardiac arrest instead of murder? Certainly not." Meadow snorted.

"Well, it does provide an opportunity to casually talk to people. It's hardly as if we can go door to door without an excellent excuse," said Beatrice, glancing around. She hoped more people decided to come, beautiful day or not.

"Whatever we have to do. I'm not going to pretend that you don't do an excellent job ferreting out bad guys in this town. All I want is for things to return to plain old boring normal." She paused. "And for Piper to have a few extra minutes for Ash to propose to him with that beautiful quilt!"

Beatrice said, "Now, Meadow. I've done what I could to help out in that respect. Piper has a very busy weekend, despite the fact that she's got a birthday. She has papers to grade and some sort of school fundraiser that she's supposed to help with. She's promised me that she's setting aside time on Sunday evening to relax." Likely with her hair in curlers and a favorite old bathrobe on, but there was no need to tell Meadow that or she'd end up staging an intervention.

"Well, I hope they both get it together and *get* together. I'm ready to play with my adorable grandchildren," said Meadow, voice growing louder with agitation.

"Adorable grandchildren?" Posy's teasing voice came from behind them. "Have I missed something?"

Meadow turned purple. Beatrice reflected again that she really couldn't seem to prevaricate. "Oh, did I say grandchildren? I meant cats."

Miss Sissy had finished haranguing Ramsay (or he had politely disengaged himself so that he could better monitor the funeral attendees) and she now stood glowering at Meadow, her good mood dissipated. "I have a cat."

Posy, a little confused over Meadow's reaction and Miss Sissy's sudden appearance said quickly, "We do, don't we, Miss Sissy. And Maisie is always so happy to go home with you."

Maisie split her time between the Patchwork Cottage and Miss Sissy's house. To Beatrice, the verdict was out whether the cat preferred the constant attention at the shop or Miss Sissy's quiet, shadowy home. But, being a cat, maybe she *was* happy at the old woman's house.

Beatrice noticed that Meadow was gesturing wildly at her. She turned slightly to see that, although the crowd hadn't increased by much, there were several of the Cut-Ups there. Although there was no sign of Orrilla Bush (Beatrice would have been surprised to see her there, considering the argument she'd witnessed), Minerva Lundy, Julia Tharpe, and Hazel Struby were all there now. They'd probably ridden together, actually. And as much as Meadow wanted her to infiltrate the group, Beatrice would much rather do so when they were apart from one another. If she tried interviewing the whole group, it would certainly set off alarm bells—alarm bells that Beatrice would prefer to keep quiet for now.

Chapter Seven

As Posy and Miss Sissy talked somewhat animatedly about the wonders of Maisie the store cat and how fetching she looked in a blue and white polka dot bow tie that Georgia had made for her, Beatrice saw the gaggle of quilters start to disperse slightly and talk to other people. Minerva Lundy was talking with Ramsay, and Beatrice couldn't tell if it were a social conversation or not. She had a smile on her face, but her eyes looked intently at Ramsay as she spoke to him.

A couple of minutes later, Ramsay was speaking with someone else and Minerva was standing by herself and looking surreptitiously at her phone. Minerva had a tendency to stand out: she was a middle-aged woman with a bob of blonde hair with an even-blonder long bang swept to the side and longer than the rest of her hair. Even though she was on her phone, she still managed somehow to look approachable. A faint smile was always on her face and the hint of a dimple. Beatrice remembered that she did a lot of volunteer work for the local parks—especially refilling the birdfeeders each week.

Beatrice said quickly, "Excuse me ladies, please," and walked toward Minerva. She could hear Meadow give a noisy sigh of relief behind her that Beatrice was going to do a little investigating.

Beatrice joined Minerva, who put her phone away with the guilty attitude of one who has their cell phone out at a funeral. "Hi," said Minerva. "Let me apologize in advance because I'm ghastly with names. It's ... Beatrice, isn't it?"

Beatrice smiled at her, "It is. And I believe you're Minerva. It's a relief to meet someone else who isn't good with names."

Minerva just smiled and nodded as if she were somewhat at a loss for what to say, or had been slightly taken off-guard by the sudden appearance of a minor acquaintance at A Serious Event.

But Beatrice had discovered in the past that knocking someone off-guard could be a very helpful exercise. "It's a very sad day today, isn't it?"

A hint of a perplexed frown showed up briefly between Minerva's remarkably unlined face before she quickly said, "The funeral? Yes. Yes it is."

It was a very unconvincing statement. Beatrice said, "You were in the same guild as Henrietta, weren't you? In the Cut-Ups?"

Minerva looked relieved as if she'd just realized a potential segue to stop talking about Henrietta and funerals. "Yes, that's right. And you're a quilter too, aren't you? My memory really is terrible. I guess you must be in the Village Quilters? Or do you just quilt completely independently of a group?"

Beatrice wasn't yet ready to get off the topic, but realized time was running short. The minister was now standing at the front of the tent of mourners. "That's right; I'm in the Village Quilters. I'm not usually much of a club person, but I've found so much support and encouragement in my guild—we're almost like sisters. You must be so very upset about Henrietta's passing. I'm so sorry."

Minerva looked as if she didn't quite know what to do with Beatrice's sympathy. "Thank you. Yes, it was very sad news. I suppose—I understand that her death wasn't an accident?"

As if Henrietta could have somehow hit herself over the head with a heavy sewing machine. "No, I'm afraid not. I know Ramsay has been going around trying to talk with everyone to get a sense of what may have happened. And to know who was at the quilt show and who might have left early. I know I left a bit early."

Minerva said sharply, "I was at the quilt show, of course, the whole time, since I was hoping to win a ribbon."

"And did you?" asked Beatrice sweetly.

They were briefly interrupted as Miss Sissy passed by on her way to the funeral home tent. The old woman hissed at Minerva as she went by.

Minerva blinked at her. "What on earth?"

"Oh, you know Miss Sissy. She sometimes gets odd ideas," said Beatrice.

Minerva looked thoughtfully after Miss Sissy, her eyes narrowed. Then she said slowly, "I did *not* win a ribbon, no."

"It was such a pity that Henrietta didn't have a chance to receive her blue ribbon," said Beatrice. "The reason I dropped by her house was to see more of her quilts. The one at the show was so stunning. She was an excellent quilter and an excellent person."

Minerva's eyes were hard as she turned to look directly at Beatrice. "She was an excellent *quilter*. Being an excellent *person* doesn't necessarily follow. There was that email, you know. That is, if you're also on the list for the mystery quilt."

"I am," said Beatrice, watching as people started taking seats under the tent. "And I didn't realize that about Henrietta. She always seemed nice. Nor did she seem like 'lying scum'."

"Seeming nice and being nice are two entirely different things. Let's just say that Henrietta wasn't the best of neighbors," said Minerva.

Beatrice raised her eyebrows in surprise. Henrietta's house was exceedingly modest and she was fairly certain that the expensive luxury car nearby was Minerva's. Plus, Minerva was wearing what appeared to be designer clothing.

"I didn't realize you lived near her," said Beatrice. She paused, thinking about Meadow and Boris and their frequent and noisy interruptions. "Sometimes a neighbor to neighbor relationship can be challenging."

"Directly next door," said Minerva coolly. "Although Henrietta had been in that house for such a long time she owned a large amount of property. It gave a sense of isolation, I guess. She also owned that vacant lot across the street from her house. I can't think why she didn't sell the land. She certainly seemed to need the money." She suddenly stopped speaking and shut her lips together tightly as if to keep more words from slipping out.

"I feel like there are two completely different views on Henrietta," mused Beatrice. "Meadow thinks she was a saint. She's always talking about how creative Henrietta was with her quilting and with her interior design work."

Minerva snorted. "Meadow is determined to think the best of everyone. Yes, she was creative and really a fine quilter and interior designer ... she did a bit of work for me at my house and I was very pleased. However, those talents do not make Henrietta a saint in any way."

"And then there are others who clearly *don't* think Henrietta was nice at all," continued Beatrice. "There was that email, of course, as you mentioned."

"I read that very spiteful email. Before you ask, I don't have any idea who would have sent out such a thing. It must have been someone deeply unhappy and bitter, judging from the tone of the email," said Minerva.

Beatrice glanced toward the minister again. He appeared to be rather uncomfortably caught up in conversation with Miss Sissy. This was buying her a little time.

"Henrietta thought it was someone who was jealous of her quilting ability," said Beatrice. "Or maybe jealous of her ribbons and awards."

Minerva shrugged, looking a bit bored. "I suppose. If you like those kinds of quilts. She certainly had talent."

Beatrice remembered Miss Sissy's conversation. "Someone mentioned that they saw you arguing with Henrietta recently."

Minerva's eyes grew frosty. "They were mistaken."

"They didn't think they were," said Beatrice. Miss Sissy was most adamant.

"Why would I bother arguing with Henrietta? It makes no sense," said Minerva, making a face.

"All right. But I was also wondering, since you live so close to Henrietta, did you see anything suspicious before she died? Did you see anyone at her house? Or were you away from home at the time?" asked Beatrice.

A slight smile twisted at Minerva's lips as she noted that Beatrice was trying to get an alibi from her. "I didn't leave the quilt show early, but I didn't stay after it was over to pick up trash or put away chairs or whatever. I saw *you* and Miss Sissy at Henrietta's house, of course."

"Yes. Unfortunately, Henrietta was already gone when we got there. Was anyone else at Henrietta's house?"

Minerva said, "Not last Friday. Although I recently saw Orrilla Bush leaving Henrietta's house. She seemed angry and stressed. I've not had a chance to ask her about it though, and now she's not at the funeral. Maybe she was mad that Henrietta wasn't paying her dues to the guild or something. It could have been something entirely innocent."

But her tone indicated that it could have been something entirely different.

It was a pleasant, basic, and very speedy service.

As it finished, Meadow said, "Over already? Goodness. Can we get over to some of the other Cut-Ups to speak with them?"

But they couldn't. The women hopped right into Minerva's car and sped away after quickly expressing their sympathy to Henrietta's sister.

Meadow and Beatrice, after seeing them leave, spoke briefly to Henrietta's sister before walking away from the group to a cement bench outside of earshot.

"Well, pooh," said Meadow. "The Cut-Ups certainly aren't making this easy on us, are they?"

"We do have the Sew and Tell on Friday, so we should be able to talk to someone then," said Beatrice.

Meadow said darkly, "If they come. I think they're being deliberately evasive. The nerve! We're just trying to find out who could be responsible so that we don't have to suspect every quilter in Dappled Hills. It's got to be one of those Cut-Ups."

Posy walked up to join them and Meadow demanded, "So who's coming, Posy? To the Sew and Tell? Any of those slippery Cut-Ups?"

Posy blinked in confusion and Beatrice quickly said, "Meadow thinks that the Cut-Ups are evading being questioned about last Friday. Although they're probably simply ready for lunch."

Posy smiled and said, "Oh, I see. Yes, I think several of them, at least, are coming. Hazel Struby is even helping with the set-up tomorrow. And Julia and Orrilla are to be there, too. I'm not sure about Minerva, though."

Meadow waved her hand dismissively at the mention of Minerva, "Oh, Beatrice has already spoken with her. Which reminds me, what did you find out?"

Posy asked curiously, "And what was Miss Sissy upset about? I thought I noticed her giving Minerva angry looks during the service."

They paused to view Miss Sissy who now seemed to be giving the minister a speech on wickedness and evil in the world. This was at a volume great enough for them to hear bits and pieces of it from some distance away. The minister was nodding nervously and glancing around for an escape route.

Beatrice sighed. "I think it's about time for Miss Sissy's nap. Who knows what she had against Minerva? She hissed at Minerva, and to me it looked like Minerva might have some sort of a hint as to why Miss Sissy was upset. She sure didn't share that hint with me, though. Miss Sissy had said that she'd seen Minerva and Henrietta arguing, but I can't imagine that was something that would make Miss Sissy that upset."

"Did Minerva seem guilty at all?" asked Meadow, eyes narrowed. "You know, she comes across all cool and collected, but I wonder if she could get mad enough or desperate enough to get rid of someone who threatened her in some way."

"Still waters run deep?" asked Posy.

"My experience has been that usually people cover up if they feel guilty. So, no, she didn't seem guilty. She wasn't a fan of Henrietta's though, that's for sure," said Beatrice.

Meadow said, "I can't believe these people! Poor Henrietta. And Minerva was saying bad things about Henrietta at Henrietta's funeral? The nerve!"

"Well, she wasn't exactly *slamming* her. Minerva would probably think that was in poor taste. But she indicated that they were not the best of neighbors," said Beatrice.

Posy said thoughtfully, "That could mean lots of things, though, couldn't it? It could mean that Henrietta didn't do a good job getting her newspaper every day and they piled up in an unsightly way in her driveway."

Meadow added, "Or it *could* mean that it was worse than that and they had a property line dispute or something."

"Minerva really didn't explain it, but she clearly felt bothered by Henrietta. Was that enough for her to murder her? Who knows? She, of course, shifted suspicion on someone else: Orrilla."

"Orrilla has been having a hard week, hasn't she?" asked Meadow.

Beatrice said, "Did you notice her arguing with Henrietta during the quilt show set-up?"

"Who *couldn't* notice it? It was very obvious. But would someone who was having all of these public confrontations with Henrietta kill her? Wouldn't that make you the most obvious suspect?" asked Meadow.

"Maybe that's why she did it—because she felt as if everyone would say that she *couldn't* have been stupid enough to murder

Henrietta after being seen in an altercation with her," said Beatrice. "Although the one argument that she had at Henrietta's house doesn't really count as public. Minerva just happened to see it. Or rather, she saw Orrilla leaving the house and looking upset."

"So who next?" demanded Meadow. "I'm thinking Orrilla should be the obvious candidate."

"Maybe she's the obvious candidate, but it's not that easy, Meadow. I can't exactly go knock on her door and demand to know where she was on Friday afternoon and whether she killed a fellow quilter," said Beatrice.

Meadow snapped her fingers. "I know what we could do! We could visit her at work."

Posy was already winking at Beatrice as if she knew that Beatrice may not *want* to visit Orrilla at work.

"Dare I ask where she works?" asked Beatrice.

"Her husband is mayor, you know," said Meadow as if she weren't going to really tackle Beatrice's question. "Ted Bush. They're a very nice family. Unless, of course, Orrilla ends up being a murderer. Isn't it funny how now *everyone*—male and female— is a 'murderer?' When I was growing up, I'd read books with 'murderesses' in them. It made them sound wickedly glamorous."

"Meadow," said Beatrice ominously, "What does Orrilla do for a living?"

"She works at a doctor's office. A very nice one that I'd certainly recommend. Wouldn't you, Posy?" asked Meadow.

"It's a very nice office," said Posy. "With a lovely fish tank to distract you from being at the doctor. And very cheerful paint on the walls. The doctors there are the best in town. Although, of course, in a small town, there's not a lot of choice."

Beatrice groaned. "A doctor's office."

"If you're thinking that would be too public a place, I can tell you exactly when we should go there," said Meadow.

Posy said, "Oh! That's right—it's always so quiet right before the office closes for lunch. That would be the perfect time to be there."

"Exactly!" said Meadow triumphantly. "Don't you need to go to the doctor, Beatrice?"

"I'm not too much of a fan of going to the doctor," said Beatrice. "And I feel very well."

"No one is a *fan* of going to the doctor," said Meadow sternly. "And the whole point of going is to ensure that you *continue* feeling better. When was the last time you had a physical?"

"It seems like just yesterday," said Beatrice with a sigh.

"Which means that it wasn't," said Meadow.

"It was a while back," admitted Beatrice.

"Goodness! Who did you see?" asked Posy.

"Doctor Wharton," said Beatrice in a low voice.

"Doctor Wharton?" asked Meadow, frowning. "Who on earth is he? I don't remember a Doctor Wharton. Did you go see some charlatan? Or ... for heaven's sake, Beatrice, was that in *Atlanta*?"

"But I've been very well," said Beatrice weakly.

"Only by the grace of God!" scolded Meadow. "All right, we do need to talk to Orrilla Bush. But we also need to get you seen by a physician. At your age, especially. Let's go tomorrow."

Beatrice said, "We can't just walk in and get a physical."

"Don't you see? This is a small town. We can head there early tomorrow morning and get your lab work done before you eat anything. While we're doing that, we can say you have a very challenging schedule (which you do with The Sew and Tell later), and ask to be fitted in right before lunch. When we're there around lunchtime, it should be very quiet and we can talk to Orrilla on the way in." Meadow stood from the bench and found her keys. "Good. We've got a plan."

And Meadow, plan in place, was now ready to leave the cemetery.

Chapter Eight

The next day, in anticipation of a doctor's visit, Beatrice skipped breakfast and coffee and had a tall glass of water instead. She found that the lack of coffee didn't much help her disposition. Noo-noo sensed that Beatrice was not in the happiest of moods and sat close to her, keeping a watchful eye. This made Beatrice smile and reach down to pet her, which in turn made her stress level go down.

"Yoo-hoo!" said Meadow's voice outside her front door. "Ready to take on your day?"

"Coming," said Beatrice as cheerfully as she could muster between gritted teeth. She gave Noo-noo one more rub for good measure. "I'll come home soon and then we'll do something fun."

Meadow had apparently had *lots* of coffee and breakfast and was full of energy. "All set? Let's tackle those medical issues!" She turned to hop back into her car.

"If there are any," said Beatrice rather mulishly, "which has yet to be established."

Meadow started up the engine and appeared not to have really listened to Beatrice. "Actually, it's good to see you this morning anyway. I can barely stand to be alone or with Ramsay. I'm just *so excited.*"

Beatrice guessed that Meadow was not referring to Beatrice's doctor's appointment or the upcoming Sew and Tell. "About Piper and Ash?"

"Yes. It's just two days away and I can hardly stand it! And Ramsay has very unkindly told me that he really can't talk about it anymore until after the engagement happens. Can you imagine?" Meadow slapped the steering wheel in frustration.

Beatrice watched as the scenery outside the car flew by just a little too fast for comfort. "That doesn't really sound like Ramsay. Are you sure you're not exaggerating?"

"I would never exaggerate! That's what he said. Although I do suppose I must have been getting ahead of myself. Just with the *topic* of my conversation," said Meadow.

"Did it have anything to do with grandchildren?" asked Beatrice dryly. "Because, considering the engagement hasn't even officially taken place, that might definitely be putting the cart in front of the horse."

"Well, maybe *some* of that. Only because our grandchildren will be the most beautiful grandchildren in the world!" said Meadow.

"And the most spoiled," guessed Beatrice.

"But I might also have been wedding planning. Just a smidge because I know that will be your territory, Beatrice."

"Actually, I believe it will be Piper's. If and when it comes down to that," said Beatrice, trying to sound a note of caution. What if Piper wasn't ready to get married yet? But it was almost impossible to slow Meadow down—she was like a speeding freight train.

"Anyway, I was just throwing around a few ideas, that's all. But Ramsay is *not* cooperative when it comes to weddings. Really, he's no help at all. I asked his opinion about two china patterns that Ash and Piper were trying to decide between and he just grunted," Meadow's face reflected her incredulity that Ramsay could be so disinterested in china.

Beatrice, who'd been looped in on this china-related debate for a while said dryly, "I'm not at all surprised that Ramsay isn't interested in their gift registry. Ash is probably having a tough time summoning up appropriate interest in their gift registry."

"Certainly not! Ash loves thinking about all the beautiful things that may be part of his new home. Even the special occasion china and the everyday china," said Meadow rather mulishly.

"For the record, which one did you prefer and I'll be sure to vote for it when I'm asked my opinion later," said Beatrice.

"Oh, I like the McKinley pattern the best for everyday. It's one of those that I don't think I'd be sick of twenty-five years later. You know, at this point in our marriage, I pull out our everyday china and I'm just *so* tired of seeing it," said Meadow. "I don't know what I was thinking of when I chose it forty years ago."

"Then I'd say you hop over to Lenoir, go into a Super Store of some kind, and buy yourself some new plates and bowls. It's not as if you can *only* get plates when someone purchases them for you at a department store," said Beatrice.

"I know I could. But then the cheap side of me says that my plates are perfectly fine and I should spend the money on something else," said Meadow with a sigh.

Meadow paused, and the speed of the car slowed too, making Beatrice vastly relieved. "I think I somehow went off on a detour with my story. At least I didn't with my driving! We need to get you to this appointment. Anyway, although Ramsay has been rather tiresome lately, he *did* do something very interesting last night. The more I think about it, the more interesting it gets."

"What's that?" Beatrice sighed as she saw the doctor's office in the distance.

"I saw that Ramsay was very focused on his laptop. And you know Ramsay: he'd usually rather stick his nose in a book. As soon as Ramsay got up to take Boris out, I peeked over at the computer. And guess what I saw?" asked Meadow.

"I've no idea," said Beatrice. She gave a small sigh as they pulled up to the doctor's office.

"A lifestyle blog!" Meadow pulled crookedly into a parking place. "You know the kind. It's sort of like reading a women's magazine—fashion tips, recipes, parenting tips and the like."

"Hmm. That does seem rather an odd choice for Ramsay. I could see him more on some sort of literature forum where readers discuss literary elements in Faulkner novels," said Beatrice.

"Exactly. So I immediately put my detective cap on and assumed it had something to do with the investigation. I mean— Ramsay. Poring over a lifestyle blog!" said Meadow. "Then I saw who the author of the blog was: our Julia Tharpe." She looked at Beatrice with a gleam of satisfaction in her eyes. "So I'm able to do some sleuthing, too!"

"All right. So Julia Tharpe has a lifestyle blog. Is that all, though? That doesn't seem like something that would make Ramsay take any interest. Lots of people have blogs, you know," said Beatrice.

"True. But this is a really *big* blog. And although I said that it was a lifestyle blog, I should have said that it really focused on just one particular niche of that area—marriage. She had articles on having a stronger marriage, ideas for fun things to do as a couple, rekindling the spark, that kind of thing. She might have had a recipe thrown in here or there, but for the most part, it was all marriage, all the time. I don't know how I didn't know about this blog. She has advertisers and sponsors and guests. I mean, this blog must actually bring in some income. It looks like a career," said Meadow. "What's more? In the sidebar of the blog it mentioned that Julia had a non-fiction book based on the blog from a major publisher that would be releasing soon."

"If she has that big of a presence, she probably *does* bring in income and it likely *is* her career. I hear that publishers sometimes offer book deals to really successful bloggers. They've got a built-in audience already." Beatrice usually would be more impatient that she couldn't see what Meadow was trying to get at, but today she was just as happy to sit in the car with Meadow instead of entering the doctor's office.

"Yes, yes, I'm sure. But look at me! I'm not even telling you the important part. I scrolled down the page to see the comments section. This blog has lots of comments on it from all kinds of people and on all kinds of posts. I think that's good 'engagement,' isn't that what it's called?"

"Meadow, the point?" Even Beatrice was wearying of this now.

"Anyway, I discovered that Julia has a troll." Meadow gave Beatrice a triumphant look. "And now we really need to go in and get your labs done."

"Wait a minute—you'll have to explain. A troll? Like the monsters that lived under the bridge when the goats were trotting over it in the fairy tale?"

Meadow said, "Not like that, no. No, a troll is a person who leaves very negative, nasty comments online. I only know this because Ash was telling me one time that the college where he works seems to have one on their blog. And Julia definitely has a troll. I could tell that the person left mean-spirited comments on various posts. Saying that Julia's marriage wasn't as happy as her blog claimed. Can you imagine? Here she's got this successful blog that teaches how to have a happy marriage and someone is leaving comments saying that it really wasn't? Julia might even have deleted some of the comments because I kept seeing *comment removed by admin*. I'm sure that's what Ramsay was looking at because why else would he have been so absorbed in Julia's blog?"

"And you think this troll is someone that Julia knows? Doesn't that seem unlikely? I'd think that most instances of this kind of thing occur when a complete stranger in the safety of his or her home is responsible," said Beatrice.

"Maybe. But not in this case. You could tell by the comments that the person knew Julia and Dappled Hills personally," said Meadow. "I think Ramsay must believe that the person behind the email about Henrietta is also the person who is attacking

Julia online. What on *earth* is this town coming to? Okay, that's enough of that. Let's head in!"

The doctor's office was as described by Meadow and Posy earlier. It was cheerful, with bright yellow walls and green chairs. There were watercolor paintings on the wall in happy tones. The music playing over the speakers was soft and upbeat.

Orrilla definitely seemed in charge. She sat behind a tall desk at the back of the waiting area and greeted Beatrice and Meadow quickly. As they approached, Beatrice saw that Orrilla seemed to be doing several things at one time—answering the phone, stapling reports, and handling the front desk. She gave every appearance of being able to handle multiple tasks well. And her hard eyes and manner made her the perfect gatekeeper to any office.

"How can I help you ladies today?" she asked briskly, continuing to staple reports.

Meadow said, "Hi, Orrilla. We're here to get Beatrice an appointment for a physical and some lab work."

Orrilla nodded and gave Beatrice and analyzing look through narrowed eyes. "Have you been here before?" was said in a voice that revealed that Orrilla did not think that Beatrice had.

Beatrice cleared her throat. It was odd how she felt as if she'd been called into the principal's office. "I haven't, no. And if today isn't convenient, I can certainly come by another time."

Meadow quickly said, "Orrilla, see if you can work her in. Beatrice hasn't been to the doctor for years and I'm desperately worried about her health."

Beatrice rolled her eyes at Meadow as Orrilla abandoned her stapling for the computer. Squinting at the screen, Orrilla said, "You're in luck. We do have some openings today. I'm assuming the lab work would be best now? It's early and I'm guessing you've fasted in preparation?"

"That's right," said Beatrice.

Meadow interrupted, "And Beatrice and I have a ferocious schedule today. Is there any way you can fit her in for that physical right before you break for lunch?"

Orrilla looked at Meadow with raised eyebrows. "There's no need for that. I've got openings available directly after the lab work is completed. That way you won't have to return later. It's all set."

"Oh boy," said Beatrice under her breath as Meadow gave her a reproving look.

Orrilla pulled out a sheaf of paper and a clipboard as Beatrice and Meadow looked glumly at each other. Then Meadow mouthed, "Go ahead! No one's here."

Beatrice said, "Actually, you're probably nearly as busy as I am, aren't you, Orrilla? Maybe you're going to Posy's Sew and Tell tonight? And, of course, you were at poor Henrietta's funeral yesterday."

Orrilla narrowed her eyes at Beatrice again, this time rather suspiciously. "I was indeed."

"Unfortunately, I didn't know Henrietta very well. As a matter of fact, I've gotten a very different impression of her recently than I had when she was alive," said Beatrice in a thoughtful voice as she took the pen and clipboard from Orrilla and stood at the reception desk to fill the papers out.

Orrilla snorted and turned to punch something into her computer. "That's probably because of that nasty email that went out. Haven't you heard? You shouldn't believe everything you read."

Beatrice felt a surge of righteous indignation because she *didn't* believe everything she read. This indignation spurred her to say, "It seems that Henrietta had the ability to make more than the emailer angry. I saw you having an argument with Henrietta at the set-up for the quilt show and someone else has mentioned that you left Henrietta's house angry recently."

Orrilla stopped typing and leveled her icy glare at Beatrice. "Let me guess. That sounds exactly like something that Minerva Lundy would say. What I've ever done to make that woman so mean to me, I've no idea."

"So you didn't have any bad feelings for Henrietta?" asked Meadow. "Because when *I* like someone, I don't jump into arguments with them at every opportunity."

Orrilla said hotly, "I had every right to be at Henrietta's house. We're both officers for the Cut-Ups. I'm the president of the guild now and she's the secretary. Or *was* the secretary. I visited strictly on guild business." But a red flush on the sides of her face seemed to refute her claim.

Beatrice said, "Are you usually angry when discussing guild business?"

"You should have tried discussing business with Henrietta! It was nearly impossible. She could be a very exasperating person. All she cared about was the art of quilting, not the business of it. Henrietta should never have been secretary," said Orrilla.

"I don't know," mused Beatrice, "from what I saw in her house, she seemed very good at writing notes."

Apparently, Beatrice's words had struck a nerve. Orrilla turned an even brighter shade of red. "I'll tell you who had something against Henrietta ... Julia Tharpe. When I was arriving for my guild meeting with Henrietta, I heard her arguing inside with Julia."

"Henrietta was arguing?" asked Meadow.

"Well, technically, I suppose it was Julia who was doing the arguing," said Orrilla.

"What could you hear?" asked Beatrice, pausing in the paperwork. She had a feeling she was writing all kinds of misinformation on the form.

"I heard Julia yelling at Henrietta that it was none of her business. That *none* of it was her business," said Orrilla.

"And you don't have any idea what she was talking about?" asked Beatrice.

"Of course not. I don't poke around in things that aren't *my* affairs. I only know that Julia was very upset," Orrilla straightened a pile of papers with more energy than needed for the task.

"Did you stay the entire time at the quilt show?" asked Meadow innocently. "Or did you leave early like so many others?"

Orrilla said, "I stayed the whole time so I could help clean up afterward. Even though we left our quilts for the week, there was still cleaning to do." This seemed to be said very pointedly at Meadow, who had the grace to blush.

Beatrice, now filling out page two of the paperwork in a very automated fashion, hoped to get the conversation away from quilt show clean up and back on to the murder. "Since you were there the whole time, you must have had a very good sense of who was there and who wasn't. Julia, for instance."

Orrilla said, "I wasn't *monitoring attendance*. I was merely there. I have no idea if Julia was there the whole time or left. Although, I did notice Minerva leaving early, as well as Henrietta. It annoyed me at the time, since many hands make light work when it comes to clean-up. I know we didn't have to leave with our quilts, since they were on display, but there was trash to take out and chairs to put away and tables to be wiped down." Again she leveled a reproachful look at Meadow, who reddened once more.

Minerva, of course, had said that she'd stayed at the quilt show the entire time—leaving only to avoid cleaning up.

"Now why don't you take a seat and finish with that paperwork while I let the lab know you're coming," said Orrilla. It was not *really* a suggestion, noted Beatrice.

"See? That wasn't so bad," said Meadow as they left the doctor's office slightly over an hour later."

"I suppose not. Although the paperwork was pretty awful," said Beatrice, climbing into Meadow's car.

"Only because you had to start over again with page one. Lots of errors due to distraction?" Meadow smiled at her as she started the car.

"I suppose. I really botched the first page, at any rate. At least that's over with," said Beatrice. "And I'm starving, so I think I'll eat half of what's in my fridge when I get home."

"And drink lots of coffee?" asked Meadow.

"My pounding head is telling me yes," said Beatrice.

Meadow said, "At least you have plenty of time before you go to the Sew and Tell to set up. I know you wanted a chance to talk to Hazel there. She's the only one I know about who's definitely helping. But tell me what you thought about Orrilla."

"She just seemed like another person who wasn't particularly keen on Henrietta. I didn't really buy her explanation about being annoyed with Henrietta because it was hard to discuss business with her. I think she was probably annoyed with her for other reasons, too. She was pretty eager to have us think badly of Minerva and Julia both," said Beatrice.

Meadow pulled into Beatrice's driveway and put the car in park. "She certainly was! Those Cut-Ups aren't very nice to each other. I think the Village Quilters is much more like a real sisterhood."

"It could just be that she doesn't want us to pay attention to *her* and what *she's* doing. Just a distraction. I know Orrilla says that she was at the quilt show the whole time, but no one was really paying attention. She could easily have slipped out and made her way over to Henrietta's house." Beatrice opened the car door and saw Noo-noo's alert face pop up through the curtains at the front picture window. Then the corgi's face grew happy and she opened her mouth in a smile.

Beatrice couldn't help but smile back. "I'll see you at the Sew and Tell, Meadow."

"Give Noo-noo some love for me!"

Chapter Nine

Beatrice not only gave Noo-noo some love, she took her on a walk … after enjoying a tremendous brunch of eggs, bacon, and pancakes. Sometimes, even when Beatrice was feeling tired, a walk was a good way to get re-energized. Even with the kind of walking that Noo-noo was fond of … stopping to smell everything and saying hi to people along the way.

After the walk, she had enough energy to take some gardening gloves and work at weeding in the backyard. There was one bed that just couldn't seem to stay weed-free. Meadow had told her that newspaper provided a good weed barrier, so she'd saved a bunch of newspapers. She spent her time moving pine needles, laying out the folded newspaper, and covering the area back up with the pine needles. Noo-noo watched contentedly. The little dog was never happier than when she was outside with Beatrice.

Before long, it was time to get ready for the Sew and Tell. The only thing was that since she'd hurried to finish the quilt for the quilt show (and was only currently working on the mystery quilt), she really didn't have anything to show right now. She supposed she'd bring the bag of fabric and her pattern and explain what her project was *going* to be.

Posy greeted them happily when she and Meadow arrived later that afternoon at the quilt store to help set-up. "Thanks so much for the help, Beatrice!"

"You know I'm happy to do it. We're setting up in the back room, I'm guessing?" asked Beatrice.

It wasn't much of a guess. The Patchwork Cottage was a lovely, cheerful shop and one of Beatrice's favorite places to go in

Dappled Hills. But there was certainly no room there for a group of quilters to work on their projects and talk about them.

"That's right. I thought we could set up the punch bowl back there and set out the sandwiches and snacks," said Posy. "I'd also really like it if we could make it look a little more intimate back there. After all, it's frequently a storage area and an office space for me when I'm not hosting a workshop."

"So maybe we could take a few of the displayed quilts and put them temporarily in the back room?" asked Beatrice.

"That would be perfect. But it would definitely be a two-person job. I could help you or Hazel—Hazel just arrived and is already in the back," said Posy. "Unless Meadow wants to help you."

Meadow wanted Beatrice to speak to Hazel, instead. "No, no, that's all right. I'll give you a hand with the chairs and food."

Beatrice said, "All right, I'll get started and recruit Hazel, too." She strode quickly enough to the back room of the shop that Maisie the store cat startled from her nap, giving her an indignant look before finally falling back to sleep in the late-day sunbeam.

Hazel was lugging folded tables from the back wall of the room to set up for the quilters and the sewing machines. She grinned at Beatrice when she spotted her. "Hi there, Beatrice! Good to see you again. And you're just in time for the heavy lifting!"

The set-up of the back room really didn't take as long as Posy thought it would. After they set up the long tables, they pulled out sewing machines and extension cords. The food table was set up very quickly with an older quilt underneath. Moving some of the quilt displays from the shop to the back room was also fast. It moved so quickly, in fact, that Beatrice was starting to worry that she wouldn't have time to talk to Hazel before the quilters arrived for the event and ruined the chance for a quiet one-on-one.

Finally, there was a moment where she and Hazel were both in the shop to see if any of the other displays would work for decorating the back room. Meadow and Posy were in the back and Beatrice could tell that Meadow was embarking on a long monologue about how happy Ash and Piper were, while somewhat awkwardly skirting the topic of their possible pending engagement.

Beatrice decided to plunge right in. "You know, after the last week, it's so good to be here in the Patchwork Cottage. My stress level drops like a brick when I walk in through the door."

Hazel gave her a friendly smile. "You too? I'm with you—this has got to be one of the most peaceful places around. It's been a bad week, hasn't it? Poor Henrietta." She had the look on her face of someone who desperately wanted to gossip and hadn't had the chance. She just didn't know that gossip wasn't what Beatrice was after. "Of course, you discovered her body, didn't you? I thought I heard that from someone. Wait—was it you and Miss *Sissy*? That must have been awful! Did Miss Sissy absolutely explode?"

"I wouldn't say she *exploded*, but she was very upset and agitated, as you can imagine."

"It's too bad that I didn't know Henrietta any better than I did," added Beatrice. "I saw her lovely quilt at the quilt show right before her death. Did you know her well? Of course, she always seemed so nice to me, but I've heard some mixed opinions of her since her passing."

"Have you?" Hazel drew closer to Beatrice. "Let me guess who might have given a mixed opinion. Maybe Minerva Lundy? I don't think Minerva really liked Henrietta all that much. It's a good thing that Minerva is a quilter and not a poker player, because you can read her feelings right there on her face!"

"And you?" asked Beatrice. "What did you think of Henrietta?"

Meadow walked up bouncily and was about to accost Beatrice and Hazel, but then saw Beatrice's quickly hidden warning look and just gave them a wave before darting back to the back of the store.

Hazel declared stoutly, "I loved her! She was one of my dearest friends."

Beatrice noticed that she looked away as she said the words, though. And that Hazel immediately switched to another topic.

"Do you know there's someone else besides Minerva who might not have liked Henrietta much? Orrilla. I could see at the quilt show that Orrilla was mad as a wet hen. She kept glaring at poor Henrietta the whole time. I wondered if maybe *she* was behind that mean email that we all got. Can you imagine sending something like that out? And under Posy's name! Posy, who does so much for us quilters." Hazel gestured so wildly in her excitement that she nearly knocked a basket of notions off a display.

"I saw them arguing at the quilt show, as a matter of fact," said Beatrice. "But I couldn't catch what they were arguing about."

"I think Henrietta must have known something bad about Orrilla," said Hazel in a very melodramatic tone.

At that point, the bell on the shop door rang and a grouchy-looking Miss Sissy came in.

"She must have driven herself here. Just watch yourself on the way home. Miss Sissy is a menace to society behind the wheel," said Beatrice with a groan.

"Hi there, Miss Sissy!" called out Hazel with a grin.

Miss Sissy glowered at her but did walk over to hover at Beatrice's elbow. "Food set up?" she inquired, a gleam in her eye.

"It's set up, but it's not time to eat it. We've got to wait until Posy gives us the all-clear," said Beatrice.

This news did not seem to make Miss Sissy's mood any brighter. She grunted and continued glowering near Beatrice.

Hazel was apparently determined to continue with her gossiping. "Since we're talking about the Cut-Ups, do you know Julia Tharpe well?"

"I wouldn't say that I know her *well*, no. I know who she is," said Beatrice.

"I was hoping you'd know her better so you could tell me what you think of her," said Hazel, looking disappointed. "She's been so odd lately. Odd enough that maybe *she's* the one who sent the creepy email."

"What about her is odd?" asked Beatrice.

Miss Sissy bellowed, "Who? Who are you talking about?"

"Julia," repeated Hazel loudly. "Julia Tharpe. You know her, Miss Sissy."

"Course I know her! Just couldn't *hear* you. Mumbling," said Miss Sissy in a fierce voice.

"Anyway, I just don't think that Julia is altogether there all the time. I've seen her twice now in downtown Dappled Hills walking down the sidewalk with a glazed look in her eyes. I called out to her and she didn't even turn," said Hazel.

"Maybe she didn't hear you," suggested Beatrice. She was never one to turn molehills into mountains unless she had more information.

"Mumbling!" repeated Miss Sissy, pointedly.

"No, she must have heard me. At least, she *definitely* heard me the second time because I was right directly in front of her, walking toward her. She looked right through me as if I wasn't there. I swear she didn't even know who I was. She almost looked as if she didn't know who *she* was. She didn't have any reaction at all to the sound of her name."

"Poppycock!" bellowed Miss Sissy.

Beatrice gave Hazel a long-suffering look. "Miss Sissy, do you know anything about Julia that you could add?"

But Miss Sissy had now become distracted by Maisie the store cat and left their conversation.

Hazel said, "You just never know when Miss Sissy is going to have a good day or a bad day. Anyway, like I was saying, Julia Tharpe was really out of it. My friend saw her another time and said she did the exact same thing. I was wondering if maybe she had early-onset dementia or something. You know? I saw a show about that on TV and it was really scary. It reminded me of Julia."

Beatrice frowned. "Well, that's good to know. If that's true, we should be keeping an eye on Julia—for her own good. But surely her husband would realize something was wrong and step in? Take her to the doctor or something?"

"Jim? I don't know if he's the most observant guy," said Hazel with a snort.

"Really? But surely he'd notice if she were acting like *that*. Besides, they seem like they have a very happy marriage," said Beatrice.

Hazel gave her an arched look. "Are we talking about the same Julia and Jim? Oh, I know—you're probably thinking about the blog, aren't you? Well, you can't believe everything you read, you know."

Miss Sissy came up to them again, cat in her arms. She said brusquely, "Food. It's time."

Beatrice glanced at her watch. "It's not quite time for it to start, but I bet everyone will be coming in in the next ten minutes. We should see if Meadow and Posy need any help downstairs. I'll just take this quilt back and if you'll take that one, Hazel? I don't think the room really needs any more decorating than that."

Hazel laughed as she picked up a quilt because Miss Sissy was already on her way. And she likely would ignore the part about it not being time for food.

The Sew and Tell seemed like a success to Beatrice, especially for the first event of its kind. Posy had organized a program of sorts and it was very personal. The quilters came in and put their quilts and notions down and got something to eat and caught up with each other. Miss Sissy was even somewhat thoughtful and didn't load her plate up with seconds, although she gave herself a very generous helping the first time around.

Posy asked if they could start and gave a very moving message about how much the shop and all the quilters meant to her while they continued to enjoy the food and punch. She asked for everyone to sign up for her email newsletter, if they weren't already on there.

After that, each quilter shared what they were working on at the time. Beatrice had thought that this section might be a bit of a wash—that maybe many of the quilters were working on similar quilts. After all, it was easy to gravitate to something that was simpler, especially during busy times. But instead, she was surprised to find that there was a lot there to inspire her. Many of the women had decided on challenging quilt patterns and their passion toward the craft was evident when they spoke about their Diced Pineapple pattern, their multi-colored Carpenter's Square, and their Northern Christmas Snowflake in red and green.

Beatrice was interested in the quilt patterns, but she was also interested in looking around at the attending Cut-Ups to see how they were doing. A killer would surely be acting somewhat differently from everyone else? But she saw little evidence of this. Minerva was there looking a bit aloof like she had during Henrietta's funeral, although she was still chatting with anyone who wanted to talk to her. Hazel was being *more* than chatty, even occasionally speaking too loudly to her neighbor as a quilter was describing her project. And Julia Tharpe had made it, too. She looked like someone with a headache, but Beatrice saw no trace of the behavior that Hazel had mentioned, even though Hazel looked pointedly at Julia and then waggled her eyebrows at Beatrice.

Maisie, the shop cat, had followed them into the back room and curled up contentedly on top of a table to watch the proceedings about as closely as Beatrice.

After everyone had taken a few minutes to talk about their projects, they all worked for a while on their quilts. Some were hand-piecing, some were working on machines. The women lightly chatted as they worked and Posy smiled happily at Beatrice. It did seem as if it turned out to be a very successful first event.

Afterward, several of the quilters talked to other quilters more about their projects and some of them moved to the shop to buy the patterns and fabric to make their own. Posy's cash register was very busy.

Meadow caught up with Beatrice and hissed, "Can you talk to Julia while she's still here? She's the only one you haven't spoken to yet."

Beatrice glanced around the shop. "Where is she?"

"Heavens! She must have left. I did see her picking up her purse, but I thought she was about to shop. See if you can catch her in the parking lot!" said Meadow.

Beatrice hurried through the other quilters, pardoning herself as she fairly sprinted out the door and to the parking lot. Halfway there, she slowed down to a walk when she saw that Julia was heading back to the shop.

"Did you forget something?" asked Beatrice.

Julia didn't look at all vague or distracted to Beatrice. Instead, she looked rather grim and deep lines creased the sides of her mouth—they didn't appear to be laugh lines, either.

"No, but my car won't start. Or rather, it won't go. Oh, I don't know *what's* wrong with the stupid thing," said Julia, sounding exasperated.

"I'm no mechanic, so I can't help you there. But you're more than welcome to ride home with me. Or, rather, with Meadow and me—Meadow drove me here. And you're a neighbor of ours, anyway," said Beatrice. "Just a smattering of woods between us all."

Julia nodded, turned to look at her car with a disgusted expression. "That sounds good. I'm definitely ready to get home. I enjoyed the event, but I'm totally worn out."

"Do you need to borrow my phone?" asked Beatrice politely.

"For?" asked Julia.

"Well, to call your husband or something. Maybe he would like to take a look at your car?"

Julia snorted. "Hardly. And I don't think he'd know what was wrong with the thing even if he *did* look at it. Besides, I have my own phone."

"In that case," said Beatrice, "Let me just run inside real quick and get my things and grab Meadow and we can head out."

Julia looked curiously at Beatrice's empty hands. "What was it that you came out for?"

Beatrice thought quickly. "Oh, I was thinking I'd get a coffee from next door since Posy had punch and I needed a little pick-me-up. I'll just get some caffeine when I get home." She hurried back into the shop.

Meadow arched her brows when she spotted Beatrice coming back in. "Back so soon? Did you miss her?"

"No, she has car trouble and you and I are giving her a ride home. Do you mind? I know we were going to help with clean-up."

Posy overheard them from the cash register. "Oh no, I've got plenty of quilters who are helping me put things away. You both helped with set-up—thanks! Now head on your way. Besides, Cork is coming later to help, too."

"Well, since her husband is coming, he can help with the heavy lifting," said Meadow. "Let's grab our stuff and go!"

A few minutes later, they rejoined Julia in the parking lot. Meadow and Beatrice put their quilts and materials into the back of Meadow's van and Julia took her things out of her car and put them in Meadow's van, too.

Meadow said, "Now you might think this is wacky, but I do actually know a little bit about cars."

Beatrice smiled at her. "I think I'd believe anything of you, Meadow."

"Do you mind if I take a look, Julia? Just for a minute, since I don't want to hold us up," said Meadow.

Julia shrugged and looked a little bored. "Feel free." And then, belatedly and a bit grudgingly, "Thanks."

"Your keys?" asked Meadow perkily holding out a hand. "Thank you!"

Julia and Beatrice watched as Meadow hopped into the car and put the key into the ignition.

"I don't really know what she can tell without looking under the hood or something," muttered Julia. "I didn't see any idiot lights go off on the dashboard or anything."

Beatrice said, "I've no idea, but I know very little about cars."

Meadow turned the key and looked intently at the dashboard. "A-*ha*!" she said triumphantly.

"Yes?" asked Julia impatiently.

"You're out of gas," said Meadow.

"Out of *gas*?" repeated Julia.

"That's right. It's an easy fix. I can drive you to a gas station and you can buy a gas can and fill it and then I can bring you back," said Meadow slowly as if Julia couldn't follow along.

Julia did seem lost in her own thoughts. "No gas. But I *swear* that I filled it up yesterday."

Chapter Ten

Beatrice looked thoughtfully at Julia, remembering what Hazel had said about dementia. She seemed so sharp, though, other than this lapse.

Meadow said, "Well, maybe you only *meant* to fill it up and forgot. Unless you have a leak in your gas tank, but I don't smell any gasoline. Should I take you to the gas station, then?"

"No, thank you. No, I'd rather Jim take care of it tomorrow sometime. We don't need to go to the trouble of lugging a gas can out here. At least I know what the problem is. Now, if you wouldn't mind taking me home? I'm exhausted," said Julia.

Meadow said, "I'm sure you are! You're doing all the quilting things and on top of it, you're working on your wonderful blog!"

A shutter fell across Julia's eyes at the mention of the blog, before she gave a rather forced grin.

They'd climbed into Meadow's van when Meadow said cheerily, "You know, exhaustion can do funny things to people. I know my memory has been in terrible state before when I was really tired. One time I went to the grocery store and was in such a fog that I left my groceries in the trunk."

Beatrice said, "That's easy to do, I think."

"Yes, but I didn't realize my mistake until the next morning when I was looking for milk to put in my cereal! I had to throw half my groceries out," said Meadow, shaking her head as she started the car.

Julia didn't seem to know exactly how to respond to this surprising declaration, so she just gave a jerk of a nod, mouth shut firmly in a tight line.

Beatrice said in a sympathetic voice (and in the hopes of having some time to ask Julia questions on the short ride home), "Who wouldn't be exhausted with the events of the last week? I've been tired myself and I barely knew Henrietta. But she was in the same guild as you, Julia. I'm sure you were both good friends."

Julia started a bit at the word *friends*. "Well, I wouldn't say we were especially close, but of course we spent a good deal of time together, being in the same guild and whatnot. She could be a little prickly sometimes, you know. But I tried my best with her. I even hired her to redecorate my house, since it seemed like she needed the money. She was a widow and I don't think she had an excessive amount to live on."

"Did she do a good job?" asked Beatrice.

Julia gave a short laugh. "When she was decorating and not messing around, she did."

"That's funny," said Meadow frowning. "Henrietta didn't strike me as the lazy type."

Julia didn't respond to this.

"I suppose sometimes you did visit with her?" asked Beatrice in an innocent voice. "I'm only saying that because someone mentioned they heard you arguing with Henrietta recently."

"They're lying then," said Julia fiercely from the back of the van. "I was at the quilt show the whole time. I didn't even find out about Henrietta's death until the next day."

Beatrice said, "I didn't mean they saw you there the same day. Perhaps the day before?"

Julia said, "That must have been Orrilla talking. Of course Orrilla would say something like that. She's trying to distract from the fact that *she* had problems with Henrietta."

"So you weren't at Henrietta's house?" asked Beatrice.

"I was. But I was merely returning a pair of shears that I'd accidentally taken home from one of the last guild meetings. I'd meant to return them to her for some time and kept forgetting," said Julia.

Beatrice said, "But you were said to be arguing with her."

"Again, that must be Orrilla Bush's interpretation of events. She's twisted things around to keep any suspicion off of her. She's the one you should be talking to, not me. I overheard a phone conversation between Orrilla and her husband when we were both in a parking lot with our windows open. I could hear her speaking perfectly and she was so engrossed in her call that she didn't even seem to realize that I was anywhere near," said Julia.

"While I was in Henrietta's house, I spotted a doodle she'd drawn on her desk. It looked like you, Julia. With daggers pointed at you. Is there a reason Henrietta would have done such a thing?"

Julia gave a startled laugh. "Not unless she was unhinged. And you're seeing something that simply isn't there. It must have been a doodle of a character that *looked* like me. It doesn't mean it *represented* me."

Meadow finally said impatiently, "Back to the point. What did you hear when you were listening in?"

"It sounded very much to me that Henrietta had found another way of making money, besides redecorating people's houses. Blackmail. From what I gathered, while Henrietta was doing her design work in Orrilla's house, she'd uncovered something about Orrilla's husband. Something that they didn't want to have uncovered," said Julia.

"Such as?" prompted Beatrice.

"Something to do with Mayor Ted?" asked Meadow with a gasp. If her local Dappled Hills government was tainted somehow with corruption, it would likely send Meadow over the edge.

"From what I could gather, it did have to do with the mayor's office. It sounded as if it were something to do with improper bids for government-related work. At any rate, it was something that would either end Ted Bush's career or possibly put him in court if it got out," said Julia in the tone of someone making a point. "So you can see why I think Orrilla might want to distract from her own involvement with Henrietta."

"Is there anyone else that you think Henrietta might have been at odds with?" asked Beatrice. "Anyone that she might have had some information on?"

Meadow asked, "Or anyone who let Henrietta work for them? Mercy. I'm so glad that I don't have enough extra money to have a decorator."

Beatrice smiled to herself. As if Meadow would have anything to hide, anyway. Aside from the proposal quilt, Meadow's life was pretty much an open book.

"Oh, I've no doubt that Henrietta could be holding something over Hazel's head," said Julia dryly.

"About *Hazel*?" asked Meadow incredulously.

Beatrice gave her a reproving look.

"If I had to guess, I'd think that Henrietta was redecorating Hazel's house (which, incidentally, could use a lot of help) and she saw something there that she knew didn't belong to Hazel," said Julia.

"How do you know this?" asked Beatrice sharply. "Did someone tell you about Hazel?"

"No. No one had to. I saw something in Hazel's house that I knew didn't belong to her. It was a phone that belonged to a friend of mine. She'd been looking everywhere for it. It had a very distinctive case," said Julia.

Meadow pulled into Julia's driveway. "But *why*? Why would she do something like that? She doesn't look like someone who needs extra money."

"I think she just *likes* to have extra money. Hazel might not be the most careful spender in the world. She likes to have fun. I think Hazel swipes things every now and then and sells them online to supplement whatever income she has," said Julia, a disdainful note in her voice.

Beatrice turned in her seat to look curiously at Julia and asked, "What did you do?"

"What do you mean?"

Beatrice said, "I mean, what did you do when you saw the phone there? Did you tell Hazel that your friend was looking for it?"

"I told her that it was so nice of her to have found my friend's phone and she would be so delighted to hear that it had been found," said Julia. "She looked very glum after that."

Beatrice said, "And you had Henrietta decorate for you, too. But she didn't try to blackmail you over anything?"

"I'm not the type of person to allow myself to be blackmailed," said Julia crisply. "Thanks for the ride."

Beatrice watched her as she strode up her driveway. "Maybe instead of allowing herself to be blackmailed, she decided to murder the source of her trouble."

"I'd believe anything right now. I think the Cut-Ups are all falling to pieces," said Meadow as she backed the van up out of the driveway and headed back down the street.

"Julia certainly seems to be," said Beatrice. "She was convinced that she had filled her car with gas."

"Oh! I remember what I was going to tell you. I took another look at Julia's blog. I can really tell a difference in the last four or five months. She used to really have it together—she posted three times a week, always on the same days. She had lots of people commenting and special events like giveaways. It looked like she had a lot of different sponsors. But in the last few months, her posting became really erratic. And, according to Ramsay, Julia had removed a couple of long, ranting blogs that people had talked about on other blogs."

"So even her behavior on the blog was different," mused Beatrice. "But what does it mean?"

Meadow said, "I guess it's what Hazel was saying. Julia may be in the early stages of dementia."

"Well, it certainly *could* be that. But it seems sort of odd, doesn't it? I'm wondering if it couldn't be something else. Because, think about it—why would Henrietta blackmail Julia over dementia? Isn't that an exercise in futility in some ways?" asked Beatrice. "It's not as if it were a condition that could be hidden for very long."

Meadow said, "But Julia said that Henrietta wasn't blackmailing her."

"Julia also said that she filled up her car with gas. I don't think we can really rely on Julia to give a clear perspective. I'm thinking that maybe Henrietta discovered something else about Julia. What if she found that Julia was taking drugs? Henrietta seems like the sort of person to go snooping around. Maybe she listened in on phone conversations and read private papers and poked around in medicine cabinets. Clearly the decorating business was a cover for her blackmailing activities. Maybe she was in Julia's medicine cabinet and discovered drugs there," said Beatrice.

"What? Like drug paraphernalia?" asked Meadow, gasping. "Or cocaine, something like that?"

"Or something much simpler. Maybe Julia is addicted to prescription drugs. That could explain the glazed look that Hazel was talking about and could explain why she got confused about the gasoline. Better yet, it would give Henrietta something to hold over Julia's head," said Beatrice.

"Except that Julia said that she wasn't the kind of person to be blackmailed." Meadow shivered.

"Which is why she might have felt pressure to get rid of Henrietta," said Beatrice.

"Julia seemed to think that Orrilla and Hazel might have something to do with it all," said Meadow. "What do you think about that?"

"I think that Orrilla might be very protective of her standing in town if she thought that someone was going to spill the beans about her husband's involvement in corruption. And I think

Hazel wouldn't be thrilled to own up to the fact that she steals things and sells them online. It's like any small town—people want to hold onto their secrets and keep others from learning about them. I can imagine all of these women giving into a blackmailer. It's tougher to imagine them as murderers," said Beatrice.

"Exactly!" said Meadow, thumping her steering wheel. "That's what I always say. I can picture them quilting, not killing."

"But I can more easily picture them getting really angry and frustrated with Henrietta and seeing red and giving her a shove. Then they could have pushed that machine on top of her once she was on the floor. Henrietta wasn't a very big woman," said Beatrice.

"Did Hazel have anything else to add?" asked Meadow. "It seemed like you were talking for a while."

"She did mention that Minerva Lundy didn't like Henrietta. But we already knew that. I wonder what Henrietta might have had on Minerva to make her dislike her so much," said Beatrice. She glanced at her watch. "All right, that's it for me tonight. I need to take care of Noo-noo and then get something else to eat since I only snacked at the Sew and Tell."

"All right. I'm tired, too. Although I don't think I'll be able to sleep a wink knowing that your daughter and my son will be engaged day-after-tomorrow!" Meadow gave a happy squeal as Beatrice got out of the van.

Beatrice hadn't had the chance to look at the weather forecast for a while and was relieved to see clear skies when she got up the next morning. It looked like the perfect day for a picnic. It would have been awful if their plans had to be scrapped again. Wyatt had texted her the night before to say he was back in town and to make sure their Saturday picnic was still on.

Beatrice had just finished getting ready when her phone rang.

Meadow's voice started without the usual greeting, "Beatrice, can you call Piper?"

Beatrice felt her heart thump in her chest. "Why? Is something wrong?"

"Yes, everything's wrong! She told Ash that she thought they should have a Monday or Tuesday night out since she felt she wasn't going to make much headway with her paper grading and logging on Sunday. She's absolutely snowed, apparently. But getting engaged on a weeknight, after they've both been working?" Meadow sounded agitated. "What's romantic about *that*?"

"I agree, but you have to keep in mind that Piper doesn't realize that she's about to become engaged. Or, rather, that she's about to be *proposed* to. She thinks they're just celebrating a run-of-the-mill birthday," said Beatrice.

"I know, I know. But can you call her? Tell her life's too short to grade papers all the time?" pleaded Meadow.

Beatrice sighed. "I don't think I can really tell her *that*, Meadow. But I can give her a call and tell her I can come over and help her grade papers and get them recorded online for her. That would likely be the best way to handle it."

Meadow sounded relieved. "Could you? Do you think you could go over now so she feels better about Sunday evening?"

"I'm about to go out with Wyatt, actually, so Sunday after church and lunch might be better. I'll call her," said Beatrice. "And now, Meadow, I've really got to go."

She hung up the phone and then dialed Piper's number. Ordinarily she didn't get involved in Piper's business, but aside from the proposal, it seemed as though she needed a lot of help right now.

"Mom?" asked Piper as she picked up the phone.

"Hi, sweetie. I was just calling to check in on you. Well, I was calling to check in with you *and* make you an offer. Meadow and I were just speaking and she was saying that you're so snowed with grading and recording grades that you don't even think you can celebrate your birthday tomorrow. I wanted to offer my help.

If you've got a sheet with all the answers, I can definitely help you grade. I can help you record grades, too. Consider me your assistant," said Beatrice with a laugh.

Piper's voice registered concern on the other end. "That's very sweet of you, Mama, but I thought you had plans for today. Aren't you and Wyatt going on a picnic? And, of course, I've got that fundraiser at the school I've got to go to."

"That's why I think tomorrow morning would be best. I'll give you a happy birthday hug and then we can get to work. We should get it all done in half the time and then you'll be free to go out for your birthday ... or stay in, either way."

Piper paused and then said, "Mama, I don't usually take a lot of help, but if you're offering, I'll take it! Thanks so much. Now please—go! Enjoy your picnic."

Wyatt had insisted on getting all of the food for the picnic himself so Beatrice really had nothing to do but to wait. And there wasn't much waiting involved—Wyatt was there on time at eleven.

He gave her a warm hug and then stood back to look at her. "Everything okay? I feel like it's been ages since I've seen you."

"Aside from murder and mayhem? It's all good. But let's just focus on our day together today. I've been looking forward to it," said Beatrice with a smile.

She grabbed her keys and pocketbook and was walking to the door when Wyatt said, "How about if we take little Noo-noo, too?"

Noo-noo's ears perked up and her mouth opened in a wide doggy smile. If she didn't exactly understand every word, she certainly got the gist of them.

"Do you mind?" asked Beatrice. "I feel as if I've seen just about as little of Noo-noo as I have of you!" She quickly put together a bag for Noo-noo with some dog food and treats and a water bottle and bowl.

They climbed into Wyatt's car, Noo-noo happily bounding into the front seat, and Wyatt drove off.

He drove to a favorite spot of theirs to walk and picnic. It had a beautiful park and wildlife area near the parking lot and a fairly easy trail that led to beautiful views of the mountain vista.

"It's so quiet here for such a beautiful day," said Beatrice with surprise.

"That's good for us! I think there are some big games on television today, so maybe everyone decided to stay home and grill and watch them," said Wyatt.

They got out of the car, Beatrice holding Noo-noo by the leash and Wyatt carrying the picnic basket and a cooler with drinks.

Beatrice asked, "Should we eat first and then walk? Or walk first and then eat?"

Wyatt said, "How about if we eat first and then walk off our lunch? That way we know we have a picnic table in case everyone suddenly decides to come out to the park. Then we can enjoy our walk and those beautiful views."

They set out their lunch on a picnic table by the sparkling pond surrounded by trees. The sun shone gently on them and there was a small breeze to keep them comfortable and to keep any bugs away.

Wyatt had brought quite a feast. There were deviled eggs, a bowl of mixed fruits, fried chicken, chicken salad mini-sandwiches, and brownies for dessert. Noo-noo settled hopefully at their feet.

"I brought something for you, Noo-noo," said Beatrice, reaching into her bag. The little dog wagged her nubbin of a tail as she saw the dog food coming out.

"Just so she isn't desperate to eat *our* food," said Beatrice with a laugh. "She's basically a stomach with feet."

"A very svelte stomach, though," said Wyatt grinning. "I'm not sure where it all goes."

"Noo-noo appreciates the compliment and hopes that her owner is paying attention! I thought she might have put on a pound or two," said Beatrice. She pulled out a drumstick. "So how was your conference?"

"It went well. I was a little nervous, as always, because I was giving a speech for one of the sessions," admitted Wyatt.

Beatrice's eyes widened in surprise. "Really? But all you do is public speaking. Well, not *all* you do, but a great deal of it. You're speaking at the pulpit or at a covered-dish-supper or at a wedding or a funeral. And you're very, very good at it."

Wyatt smiled at her. "Thanks for that. Somehow, when I'm speaking in front of a group of other ministers, especially a *large* group of other ministers, I still get nervous. I solved the problem by getting there early, making sure the microphone and the slideshow worked, and greeting everyone as they came in. It put me more at ease."

"That's a good way to do it," agreed Beatrice. "And I'm sure you had a great presentation—you always put so much effort into everything you do."

They sat in a contented silence for a minute, watching the trees sway gently in the breeze. A few geese landed into the pond with barely a ripple. Noo-noo munched away below them.

Beatrice asked curiously, "Out of curiosity, where do you see yourself in a few years? Doing more speaking at conferences? Retiring? Continuing at the church? Any dreams for your future?"

Wyatt hesitated and then said lightly, "I haven't completely decided yet. There will probably be a few considerations I'd need to keep in mind."

"Oh, goodness, I know what you mean. When I was looking at retirement from the art museum, there was so much to consider it was overwhelming! Did I have enough to live on? Did I want to live in Atlanta or live near Piper? What about healthcare? Did I want to downsize into a smaller place?" Beatrice shook her head ruefully.

She was about to go on to say that *all* life changes were like that. Beatrice thought about mentioning Piper's proposal to Wyatt, but then she stopped herself. She had no doubt that Wyatt would be completely discreet—that, after all, was a big part of his job as a minister. But part of her thought that no one else really needed to know about the proposal before Piper herself did. And if Meadow could keep a secret—even though she was looking like she was about to pop under the weight of keeping it—then Beatrice could, too.

Fortunately, Wyatt was talking and didn't seem to notice her dilemma.

"Do you have any dreams for your future, Beatrice?" he asked.

Beatrice gave a short laugh. "Right now, the dreams all entail spending a quiet afternoon in my hammock with an excellent book, a glass of white wine, and Noo-noo snoring beside me."

Wyatt grinned at her. "That's pretty much the impossible dream, isn't it?"

"It might as well be! Not only do I get foiled by Meadow and quilting obligations, but I really think I'm my own worst enemy. I have a hard time relaxing."

They spent the next thirty minutes finishing the delicious lunch and talking about their favorite books now and their favorite books growing up. Beatrice was pleased to find that she and Wyatt had lots in common with their reading.

Noo-noo was asleep on her back with her feet in the air, giving Wyatt and Beatrice something to chuckle over.

"We should go on our walk or else we'll end up sacked out like Noo-noo," said Beatrice wryly as they threw away their trash, put away the remaining food, put a halter and leash on Noo-noo, and headed for the trail.

"Do you want to take a stroll around the pond first?" asked Beatrice. "The trail isn't exactly strenuous, but maybe I should still work up to it after all I ate."

"Besides, the pond is beautiful today with the sun and clouds reflecting in the water. Good idea," said Wyatt.

The path next to the pond took them through some wooded areas. The park had been designated a wildlife habitat. There were birdfeeders, birdbaths, and birdhouses scattered through the park. It was quiet there still, with a lone fisherman on the other side of the pond.

They were chatting lightly, Noo-noo keeping a peppy pace for the walk, despite all that she'd eaten. But the corgi stopped short suddenly, staring into the woods ahead with concern.

"Something wrong, Noo-noo?" asked Wyatt, frowning. "Is it just a squirrel or something?"

"She wouldn't be upset over a squirrel," said Beatrice. "Maybe there's a stray dog in there. That would give her pause. Should we hold back?" The idea of tangling with a stray wasn't very appealing.

"But I'm not hearing any leaves rustling," said Wyatt.

Beatrice prompted Noo-noo to go and she moved ahead. Now she was straining at the leash, wanting to show them something or find out more about something.

"Is that something there? On the ground ahead?" asked Beatrice suddenly. She tightened her grip on the leash to make sure Noo-noo didn't get too close.

They approached a spot in the strip of woods between the path and the pond. There was a birdhouse there and a nearby birdfeeder. And, lying crumpled forward on the ground was a woman's body.

Chapter Eleven

Beatrice automatically handed the leash to Wyatt. "I'll see if she's all right. Can you call Ramsay?"

Beatrice moved cautiously forward, trying not to disturb any potential evidence in case there was foul play. She crouched on the ground at peered at the woman's face and then sighed. Beatrice reached out to feel for a pulse and then said, "Tell Ramsay it's Minerva Lundy. She's dead." She glanced to the side as a metal object caught her eye. "It looks as if she's been hit on the head with a heavy wrench."

Wyatt was grimly speaking to Ramsay as Beatrice made her way carefully back to the path.

"He's on his way," said Wyatt quietly. They both stared at the slumped figure and then Wyatt gave a brief but heartfelt prayer.

After a moment or two, Beatrice said, "As I recall, Minerva was a volunteer for the park."

"That's right. She filled the birdfeeders each week."

Beatrice said, "So, unfortunately, her schedule was probably known by everyone. It would have been easy for someone to wait for her out here. In fact, they'd have known she'd be making the rounds between feeders and they probably chose this one carefully. It's more heavily wooded here and would afford the killer more privacy."

Wyatt said, "The location makes sense. What *doesn't* make sense to me is the fact that someone would want to kill Minerva. It must somehow be tied into Henrietta's murder. There couldn't be *two* murderers on the loose in Dappled Hills."

"I'm sure they're tied in. But I've no clue why someone would want to murder Minerva. It didn't seem to me as if she knew something when I spoke to her. She was basically blaming everyone else, saying that Henrietta wasn't the most popular of guild members. But she must have known or seen something or else why would she be a danger to the murderer?" asked Beatrice.

Ramsay was there within minutes and looking grim. "Over here?" he asked, pointing to the woods. A couple of moments later he said, "Okay. Tell me what you know. I've got Lieutenant Thomas and his team on the way and until then I need to stay close to the body. Let me get a statement from you and then the SBI can contact you if they have any additional questions."

They filled him in quickly. "Really, we don't know very much," admitted Beatrice.

Ramsay sighed. "I blame myself for this. Minerva mentioned at Henrietta's funeral that she wanted to talk to me. I tried to schedule a time with her yesterday, but she said she had too many conflicts. I wonder if someone overheard our conversation or realized that Minerva looked as if she knew something."

"She didn't tell you why she wanted to talk to you?" asked Beatrice.

"No, she was trying to downplay it. But whatever it was, I think it was more important than she was making out." Ramsay paused and appeared to try to gather his thoughts. "You didn't see Minerva when you arrived or while you were here?" asked Ramsay.

"No. As a matter of fact, we didn't really see *anyone*. We were amazed at how quiet it was out here on such a pretty day. We did see a fisherman, but that's all," said Beatrice.

Ramsay nodded. "And that fisherman hasn't moved, either. You didn't see anyone *leaving*? Anything suspicious?"

Beatrice and Wyatt shook their heads.

"All right. Looks like we'll have to figure out what we can in the lab." Ramsay sighed. "She seems to me like she might have been here for a little while. Especially if you didn't even see her arrive."

"You saw that wrench beside her?" asked Beatrice.

"I did. We'll assume that's the murder weapon, although I think our killer would be too smart not to wear gloves or to wipe prints off the weapon," said Ramsay. "We'll see what we can get." He paused and looked wryly at the two of them. "Not the way you planned for your picnic to go, was it?"

"Not at all," said Wyatt with a sigh.

After speaking with Ramsay, Wyatt and Beatrice headed to the car. The park was going to be closed off while the police made their investigation so there was no way to have their walk.

"I'm sorry," said Wyatt in a regretful voice.

"I'm sorry, too," said Beatrice as they climbed into the car. "I was looking forward to this and it was such a beautiful day."

"I'm sorry about Minerva, too. I'll need to make plans to contact Minerva's husband, Benjamin, to extend my sympathy after the police have informed him," said Wyatt.

Beatrice said slowly, "I'm sure the police will likely want to work in a few questions, too. Considering that husbands are usually the most likely suspects." She paused. "What do you know of their relationship?"

Wyatt shook his head. "I know nothing of it in a pastoral sense, and of course I wouldn't be able to reveal it if I did. Although I thought I'd noticed some tension between Minerva and Benjamin on a previous occasion. That's hardly abnormal for marriages, though."

Beatrice absently stroked Noo-noo who was lying quietly in her lap as they rode back home. "She was Henrietta's neighbor, of course. And now they're both gone. I wonder if she *did* see something and the murderer knew she had."

He shook his head. "I hate to think that someone would do that. But this was clearly no accident. And Beatrice—I know that you have a knack for figuring these things out. But please promise me you'll be careful."

Beatrice reached out and touched his free hand gently. "I will."

After Wyatt had dropped Beatrice off, she found that she was too restless to be able to sit still. She pulled on some walking shoes, grabbed a leash, and took happy Noo-noo for a walk. She was walking past Meadow's house when Meadow came hurrying out. "I spotted you from the kitchen window!" she called. "Come on in!"

Noo-noo heaved a large sigh as they headed toward Meadow and Beatrice paused and leaned down to give the little dog a reassuring pat. "Boris will be better-behaved at his own house. And we'll finish our walk soon."

Meadow was in something of a tizzy when they walked in. Her home was filled with a mouth-watering aroma. She appeared to be in the midst of a baking frenzy. "Ramsay finally told me what was going on after I called him a few times and left messages. How awful! It's unnerved me so much that I've thrown myself into baking. Here, have a banana nut muffin. And Noo-noo, a treat for you, you poor dog! Finding bodies on your walk! Brave little corgi!" Her voice cracked a bit as she tossed a biscuit to Noo-noo. "Down, Boris! No!" she said to the huge dog as he tried to snap at the biscuit in mid-air. Then she compensated by giving him one of his own.

"Noo-noo is very observant. She knew right away that there was a problem and was sure to alert us about it. I don't think Wyatt and I would have noticed Minerva lying there. She was off the path and nearly hidden in the strip of woods bordering that part of the lake," said Beatrice.

Meadow stirred a new batch of batter viciously with a wooden spoon. "So it sounds like she was at the park, filling birdfeeders, minding her own business and someone was lying in wait for her?"

"It somehow sounds even more nefarious when you put it that way, but yes. Someone obviously knew her routine and likely waited for her at that particular spot at the park. It was pretty secluded with good tree cover. And ... they brought a wrench with them," said Beatrice.

"Wickedness!" spat Meadow, sounding very much like Miss Sissy. She tossed another muffin on Beatrice's plate and shoved a glass of milk her way.

"I suppose Minerva followed a very set routine?" asked Beatrice. "I didn't really know her well, although she seemed very organized."

Meadow said, "Minerva was somewhat of a creature of habit. You could set your clock by her, really. She'd go to Posy's shop the same day every couple of weeks to see what was in stock. She'd go to the park every Saturday and Wednesday, always at the same time, to fill the feeders and maybe clear any large sticks that might have fallen in the path. She was a regular at the breakfast restaurant downtown and always had breakfast there on Friday mornings."

"She made it easy for her killer then," said Beatrice.

"At least we know now that she wasn't involved in Henrietta's death." Meadow greased a muffin pan with a good deal more force than was required for the task.

Beatrice said, "Well, we really don't *know* that. I suppose that she could have been involved in it and then someone killed Minerva for revenge. But considering we know that Henrietta wasn't the most popular of people, that does seem unlikely. It's much more likely that Minerva saw or knew something that Henrietta's killer wanted to keep quiet."

"So who do we see first?" demanded Meadow as she poured batter into the greased muffin pans. "I'm ready to go get this murderer locked away for good."

"I don't think we can just go door to door and give people the third degree," said Beatrice, reaching for a napkin.

"Maybe we can give *Miss Sissy* the third degree," said Meadow thoughtfully.

"Miss Sissy?"

"Remember? You said that Miss Sissy didn't seem to like Minerva for some reason. That she was making noises at her at Henrietta's funeral. Maybe Miss Sissy knew something about Minerva," said Meadow.

"Maybe she does. But getting information from Miss Sissy isn't all that easy. I don't know. I feel like we have all these different bits and pieces of the puzzle and we don't know how any of them fit together. Julia's mean blog commenter, Miss Sissy's dislike for Minerva. Hazel's thievery." Beatrice sighed.

The back door opened and a weary Ramsay came in. He smiled at Beatrice when he spotted her. "Ah, Beatrice and Noo-noo. You've both had the same sort of day that I have." Noo-noo trotted over happily to him and Ramsay rubbed her tummy as she flopped down on the wooden floor in front of him.

"You're already done over there?" asked Meadow, hands on her hips. "Does that mean that the killer is arrested and behind bars? Because I'm not feeling all that safe in my hometown right now. Really, I don't know how I'm expected to sleep tonight when I might be murdered in my bed."

Ramsay washed his hands in the kitchen sink, drying them with a paper towel. "No, my being home means that I can't find any more information right now. It's sort of a waiting game. The state police have taken Minerva to their crime lab and checked the area looking for clues to the killer's identity. All I could do was to observe what I saw at the crime scene. There was no one there to question, no statements to take besides Wyatt's and Beatrice's, which I got. Unless you want me to start asking Noo-noo questions, I think I'm done for the next hour. And I need an hour to think before I start asking questions of my usual suspects to find out where everyone was during the murder."

Beatrice gave Ramsay a sympathetic look. "I'm sorry. This is sort of the worst case scenario for you, isn't it?"

"Well, it's much worse for Minerva, but yes. Investigating serious crime isn't exactly what I thought I'd be signing up for in Dappled Hills." Ramsay sighed and reached for some muffins. Then he looked hopefully at Beatrice. "I know I recently gave you a book to read, but would you be interested in reading any of my short stories? I've written several lately."

Beatrice knew that Ramsay would stray far away from crime investigation and completely embrace reading and writing literature if he had the chance. She smiled at him. "I'd love to."

Ramsay walked over to the kitchen table and delved into a mish mashed stack of unruly papers. "Here! Enjoy."

Beatrice took them and smoothed the wrinkles out, gently. "Thanks. I'll get them back to you very soon and in good shape."

Meadow snorted from the stove where she appeared to now be preparing vegetable omelets. "Don't worry about that! Ramsay has oodles of copies of those short stories lying around. And they're not in good shape to begin with."

"Well, except for that bottom one," corrected Ramsay. "That's actually the only copy of it."

"You don't even have a copy on your computer?" Meadow asked.

"No, I wrote that one longhand. It just felt right to do it that way," said Ramsay.

Beatrice hid a smile. Ramsay the artist.

Meadow asked, "Have you heard back from those magazines and whatnot? Whatever it was that you were sending them to?"

"Not yet," admitted Ramsay. "But maybe I'll hear soon. I understand that these literary magazines have a lot of stories to comb through. And I sent them to a lot of different places."

Beatrice said with a smile, "I'm sure they'll get back to you soon. I'm looking forward to reading them."

Meadow pulled a plastic bag out of the cabinet under the kitchen sink. "Here! You'll want to make it easier to carry them, since you're on a walk." She snapped her fingers. "And pooh! I wanted to give you your philodendron to take back home. I don't suppose you can carry a plant along with the short stories and still manage the leash?"

Beatrice put her hands up. "I've already got a losing record with that plant, so I better not risk it."

"All right, I'll drop it by the next time I think about it," said Meadow.

There was a tap on the door, making Ramsay frown. "We weren't expecting any company, were we?"

Meadow said in a forceful voice, violently flipping an omelet, "It better not be some citizen advising you of another dead quilter."

It was Ash. And seeing him come through the door made Meadow abandon her stove altogether. "Ash! Oh, it's so good to see you! And right before your momentous occasion, too." Tears came into Meadow's eyes and she choked up a bit on the last words.

Ramsay rolled his eyes at Beatrice as Ash gave Meadow a comforting hug. Ramsay said to Beatrice, "I'll see you in a while."

Ash waved to his father and then came over to hug Beatrice too as Meadow resumed her omelet station. "Thanks for all your help with the quilt." Meadow loaded a plate with everything from muffins to veggie omelets and shoved it and a fork his way.

Beatrice said, "It was an honor. Of course, you know, I just couldn't be happier for you and Piper."

Ash laughed as he picked up a fluffy muffin. "It'll be really awkward if she turns me down after all this, won't it?"

Meadow said, still wiping away a stray tear, "As if she would. Although it might be harder getting a chance to *see* her. Apparently, her birthday weekend has been jam-packed with work-related stuff."

"I'm actually helping Piper out tomorrow," said Beatrice. "I thought that might be the best way to make room on her calendar." She didn't mention that part of her mission might be to get her daughter out of exercise clothes and into something dressier for the occasion.

This time Meadow hugged her. "Thanks for helping!"

Beatrice said, "And now I think it's time for Noo-noo and me to finish our walk. I think she's wondering why I promised her a walk and ended up with a visit."

"Sweet Noo-noo," said Ash, gently petting the corgi. She grinned up at him.

Meadow said, "Before you go, you never answered my question from earlier. Who do we see first? Which suspects?"

Ash shook his head, put his now-empty plate in the dishwasher, and headed toward the back, "I'm going to check in with Dad real quick."

"Who do *you* think we should see?" asked Beatrice, feeling a bit weary. Or maybe just a little sleepy after all of the food.

"Hm. How about if we start back with Orrilla again?" said Meadow.

"Orrilla? How are you planning on doing that? Do *you* need a physical?" asked Beatrice.

"No, I had mine months ago." Meadow snapped her fingers. "I know—you could say that you had some trouble understanding your bill and wanted to ask some questions about it."

Beatrice frowned. She didn't like this idea much at all. It horrified her that anyone would think she couldn't understand a very simple and straightforward bill. "And run by the doctor's office with it? That seems ridiculous."

Meadow shrugged. "It's a small town. People do things like that here. I tell you one thing; it's a lot better than calling up those 1-800 numbers for customer service. Half the time you have to punch a million numbers to reach a customer service person. Then they want you to talk to a robot! And then, if you *do* get someone, you've had to wait on hold for thirty minutes. When they finally pick up, it's someone from another country and you can't understand a word they say!" She pushed dishes haphazardly into the dishwasher with a disgusted clatter.

Beatrice blinked at the rapid change of subject. "Yes, annoying. But on to Orrilla."

"Yes. We could go see her tomorrow. Right after you help Piper with the grading and so forth. I could use something to occupy my mind in the meantime. I'm so wound up about the pending engagement that I won't be able to sit still!"

Beatrice could picture it now—she and Meadow harassing poor Orrilla over a basic billing statement while Meadow was restlessly pacing the room like a caged lion. She groaned.

"Meadow, tomorrow is Sunday, by the way. Surely you're not suggesting we go visit Orrilla at home."

Now it was Meadow's turn to blink in surprise. "Well, of *course* I am. We've got to get a move on this case!"

"We simply cannot knock on Orrilla's door on a Sunday afternoon to complain about a very easy bill! I can't be a party to that, Meadow."

Meadow sighed. "All right. Maybe you aren't the most likely candidate for not understanding your bill. Oh, wait! I know. We could drop by and say that we're collecting for the Red Cross. Then, if she gives us money, we can donate it online."

"It's better than your first idea, for sure. Is that something you usually do?" Beatrice couldn't remember Meadow collecting door-to-door before.

"No. But why not? It's a good cause and a good excuse," said Meadow.

Chapter Twelve

Noo-noo seemed happy to continue her walk. She picked up a fast pace and led Beatrice on a path to much more exercise than she had expected.

When Beatrice's phone rang, she was breathless when she picked up. That's when she decided to turn the little dog around to head back in the direction of home.

"Mama?" asked Piper.

"Yes?"

"Well?" she demanded, a laugh packed into the word.

Beatrice frowned. "Well? Sorry, well *what*?" She was starting to get the sinking sensation that perhaps Piper had somehow caught wind of her upcoming proposal. Or did Beatrice forget what time she was helping with the grading? "Wait. I wasn't supposed to come help you *this evening*, was I? I'd thought we'd arranged for tomorrow morning."

"No, no. Tomorrow is great. Or not, if you have other things to do. I was just calling to find out how it went."

Beatrice was truly puzzled now. "How what went?"

There was a pause on the other end of the phone now. Piper said slowly, "Didn't you go on the picnic this morning?"

"Oh, the picnic." Piper clearly hadn't heard about them finding Minerva's body. But then, if she was at a fundraiser for a school or holed up grading papers, it was really no surprise. "Actually, Noo-noo and I are walking right by your house. How about if we pop in for just a few minutes? Then I do need to head back and feed her."

Beatrice was glad to tell Piper in person. It would keep her from feeling nearly so alarmed to see that Beatrice really was fine, although she'd had a scary experience. She explained the situation just as soon as she and Noo-noo came in. "I won't sit down, this time. We'll get a better visit in tomorrow morning. Noo-noo and I had something of a rough morning. We had our picnic and it was lovely—Wyatt had even invited Noo-noo along and she was pleased as punch. He'd packed wonderful food, the weather was nice, and hardly anyone was there. But after we ate, Wyatt, Noo-noo, and I took a stroll around the lake to sort of warm ourselves up before hitting the trail. And we discovered—or, rather, Noo-noo discovered—Minerva Lundy's body."

Piper gasped and put her hands to her face. "No!"

"I'm afraid so. It seemed like the murderer knew her routine and was waiting for her in a more secluded area on the path. So we never went on our walk, of course, since Ramsay and the state police needed to try and collect evidence and treat the park as a crime scene," said Beatrice. "It was definitely not what we'd expected."

Piper shook her head. "And it's so hard to believe. Minerva always seemed very self-contained and kind of ... removed. It's hard to imagine her being murdered, or even taken off-guard. And I'd think she would have fought back, too. She had that kind of scrappy personality."

"Well, I think she likely *would* have fought back, but the killer didn't appear to give her an opportunity. From what I could see, she was hit on the back of the head with a very heavy wrench. In that respect, I guess, she was lucky. She probably never knew what hit her and wouldn't have been afraid. She was simply out following her usual routine and doing something she enjoyed," said Beatrice.

Piper said, "Mama, you just keep getting so close to these murders. I worry about you. Promise that you'll be careful."

"You know I will. And at least Wyatt was with me today."

"Although not exactly what y'all had planned," said Piper, making a face.

"Well, the picnic was nice, at least," said Beatrice.

Piper reached down to pet Noo-noo. She said, "You know, maybe I should do my own grading tomorrow and let you have a quieter, less-stressful day. Why don't you try to reschedule with him instead?"

Beatrice shook her head. "You know how busy Sundays are for him. He's got the services and then he usually leaves church to go straight to Lenoir to the hospital to visit all the sick church members. He'll probably be ready for a nap after all of that instead of seeing me. No, let's stick with the original plan. And now I'd better get Noo-noo back home. I'm sure she's been thinking what a weird walk we've had, and she's got to be starving."

Piper smiled. "Give her an extra treat today for her scary morning. And I'll see you tomorrow. Thanks, Mama."

Noo-noo ended up getting a couple of extra treats, to her great excitement. Beatrice turned in and slept surprisingly well, considering her day.

The next morning she was over at Piper's house early. She was glad to see that, instead of the sloppy clothes Piper had told her she'd be in, she was actually in a very classic pair of comfortable black pants and a flowing black and white blouse.

It took Beatrice a little bit longer to figure out exactly what Piper needed to get done than she had expected. There was no grade book; instead, they needed to digitally record the grades on a site that was shared with the students and parents. Once Beatrice had figured out what to do, the work went quickly. And she was rewarded with a big hug from Piper.

In fact, they were done much earlier than Beatrice had thought they'd be. She called Meadow when she got home.

"You're done?" asked Meadow, who sounded like she might be eating her lunch.

"Finished early. It was a little tough to figure out at first, but once we got going, it went quickly. Want to do our Red Cross collection scheme?" asked Beatrice.

"Absolutely!" said Meadow. "I'm just finishing up lunch now. Let me put on a believable outfit."

Beatrice wondered what a believable Red Cross outfit for Meadow would entail. She found out minutes later when Meadow showed up in a pair of white pants and a red top. "What do you think? Perfect, isn't it?"

"It's red and white, that's for sure," said Beatrice. She was, as usual, wearing her own daily uniform of a pair of khaki pants and a crisp button-down shirt.

"You don't think it would look suspicious if I put her donation in my purse, would it?" asked Meadow, heading back out to her van.

"Well, I don't think it would look very official. And official is what we're shooting for, isn't it?"

Meadow said, "Do you have something I can put our collection in?"

"Let me grab a manila envelope," said Beatrice with a sigh. "Ramsay hasn't made any progress with finding out alibis, has he? It could save us some trouble."

"He was gone quite a while yesterday evening and I'm sure he and that Lieutenant Thomas were talking to suspects. But he came back in such a grouchy mood and so tired that he wouldn't give me *any* information when I asked him. It looks like we're on our own," said Meadow, sounding put-out.

Minutes later they were knocking at Orrilla's door. In fact, Meadow was about to impatiently knock again.

"For heaven's sake," fussed Meadow under her breath. "If we're going to go to all this trouble, the least she can do is to be at home when we're here."

Beatrice said, "We didn't exactly ask her to RSVP, Meadow. This was supposed to be a spur of the moment thing."

The door finally opened and Orrilla stood there, not looking particularly happy to see them there. "Yes?" she inquired.

Meadow beamed at her as if Orrilla was her long-lost friend and she was delighted to see her. "Hi! Beatrice and I are collecting for the Red Cross. Can you help out?"

"Um ... "

Beatrice said, "Of course she will! Orrilla is such a helpful person."

Orrilla looked doubtfully at Beatrice.

"You were very helpful in the doctor's office with the last minute scheduling and everything," said Beatrice.

"I may be able to give a little something," said Orrilla rather grudgingly.

She turned as if to get her purse and was in the process of closing the door back on Meadow and Beatrice when Meadow said brightly, "Okay if we come in? I'm dying for a glass of water. Collecting money is a very thirsty business."

Orrilla made some sort of concessionary grunt that was muffled in a grumble.

Meadow plopped down in Orrilla's living room as if she were exhausted from walking all day. "Whew! Collecting money is tough work," she declared loudly.

Orrilla returned with what looked like a couple of dollar bills and thrust them at Meadow, who complacently stuck them in her envelope. Orrilla paused for a second as if hoping that Meadow would forget her request for water. But Meadow continued her unwavering cheerful smile at Orrilla. Finally, Orrilla gave up, walking stiffly to the kitchen.

She returned a moment later with a glass half-filled with water and no ice.

Meadow, who was supposed to be very thirsty, dutifully gulped some of it down. She looked at Beatrice as if prompting her to get going with the interview.

Beatrice cleared her throat. "You know what I think? We're so exhausted because of yesterday. Isn't it so awful, what happened to Minerva?"

"I heard that you were the one to discover Minerva's body," said Orrilla in a disapproving voice. "Just as you were the one to discover Henrietta. What an unfortunate habit you have."

Beatrice somehow felt as if Orrilla was somehow blaming her for the deaths of Henrietta and Minerva. She gritted her teeth in a smile and continued. "Bad luck, is what it was. Clearly, you've already heard the news about Minerva."

Orrilla shrugged. "News travels fast in a small town."

"Were you here at home yesterday morning?" asked Beatrice.

Orrilla shook her head, looking away. "No, I wasn't. I was at the library. Sometimes I like to go there to read or balance my checkbook. I heard about Minerva after I'd gotten home."

Meadow said, "What amazes me is all the bad blood in the Cut-Ups! Who might have been that upset with Minerva to kill her?"

Orrilla rolled her eyes. "There wasn't 'bad blood' in the Cut-Ups. There were only a couple of squabbles here and there. It's not the same thing. I don't know what happened to Minerva, but no one in our guild hated her or was out to get her. She just occasionally rubbed people the wrong way. Minerva was attractive and had a lot of money and was somewhat of a flirt."

"Did she flirt with your husband?" asked Beatrice.

This made Orrilla laugh out loud. "Not with *my* husband, no. Not with Ted."

Meadow made a face at Beatrice to indicate that Ted Bush wasn't exactly someone to write home about.

Beatrice knew, of course, who Orrilla's husband was, but that was only because he was the mayor. He wasn't especially good-looking, that was true, but maybe women were attracted to the fact that he was in a position of power? Although it wasn't much power, considering it was tiny Dappled Hills. That's when

Beatrice remembered that there was something she *did* know about Orrilla's husband that Julia had mentioned.

"Speaking of your husband, did you want to clear up any misunderstandings related to him?" asked Beatrice.

Meadow took another gulp of her tepid water.

Orrilla turned an unattractive shade of purple. "Misunderstandings?" she gave a short laugh. "I don't know what you're talking about."

But her flush betrayed her. Beatrice said, "Something to do with Ted considering improper bids for town-related work?"

Orrilla's mouth opened in a snarl. "Who have you been talking to? That's a vicious lie. Worse than a lie—it's libel."

Chapter Thirteen

Beatrice raised her hands in front of her in a 'calm down' gesture. "I didn't mean to provoke such a response, Orrilla. I was only letting you know what people were saying and giving you a chance to explain."

"There's nothing to explain! And our visit is over. You can both take your money and go." With that, Orrilla stormed out of the living room, abandoning her guests to find their own way out.

"Well, that certainly didn't take up the rest of the afternoon like I'd hoped," said Meadow. "Pooh."

"I didn't think she was going to explode like that. If I'd known, I'd have approached the question more carefully and at the very end of our visit. It definitely cut our interview short," said Beatrice as she climbed into Meadow's van.

"And you know what that tells me?" demanded Meadow. "It tells me that it's true. That Mayor Ted *did* do something that was unethical. The mayor! Fiddling with bids for town work!"

Beatrice said, "It also tells us that Orrilla was violently opposed to having people find out about the problem. Maybe she was violently opposed enough to actually shut someone up permanently."

"This is all very upsetting. You start thinking that everyone in your town is crooked!" Meadow's expression was dark. "And I know exactly what I want to do now."

"Dare I ask? You look as if you want to round up half the town and stick them in jail," said Beatrice.

"I want to go downtown to June Bug's shop and eat a cupcake. It's Sunday afternoon and I've just lost faith in my mayor and I want a cupcake," said Meadow, emphasizing every word.

That did, actually, sound very good. Not only because Beatrice felt as though she could use a shot of sugar, but because she liked supporting June Bug, who had to be the hardest-working person in Dappled Hills. Not only did she bake cakes for both her shop and for special occasions, she somehow found the time to make incredible and inventive quilts.

"Let's go," Beatrice said with a smile.

Beatrice took a deep, appreciative breath as they walked into the bakery. She smelled the sweet scent of muffins, cakes, and cookies. When Meadow and Beatrice helped June Bug move in, they'd tried to make the shop as cheerful and cozy as possible and had draped quilts around the shop to help set the tone. June Bug had also shyly asked some fellow quilters if they'd like to put some of their quilts for sale in her shop, so there were some on display with price tags attached. Business seemed to be booming.

Beatrice was glad to see Savannah and Georgia in the shop. The other quilters were sure to help rid Meadow of her stormy expression.

"Sit down with us!" called Georgia. "Savannah and I were hoping for some company and June Bug is too busy to visit."

Beatrice was glad to see that June Bug was that busy. The shop was indeed full of customers and she was hopping around taking orders and money, making change, and getting cakes and cupcakes out. The phone was ringing as well.

"Isn't this *lovely*?" asked Meadow. "Who knew that Sunday afternoon would be a busy time for a sweetery?"

June Bug's round face had a big smile when she spotted Beatrice and Meadow in line.

"What'll you ladies have?" she beamed at them as they finally got to the front.

"A chocolate cupcake!" said Meadow. "Actually, make it two. It's been a rough week."

"And for you, Beatrice?" asked June Bug, multitasking as she spoke.

"What's new? I'd ask 'what's good,' but since you've made everything, I *know* it's all good." Beatrice leaned in to see the selection in the glass counter.

"Maybe the walnut carrot cupcake with orange cream cheese frosting?" suggested June Bug.

"That sounds amazing, June Bug. Let me have one of those. Actually, could I also have two to go?" asked Beatrice.

As June Bug was industriously getting their orders together, Meadow said, "Some now, some later? That's good of you to portion it out. No wonder you're so slim!"

"I wasn't really keeping my diet in mind. Although it wouldn't hurt me to do so," said Beatrice wryly. "I was mainly thinking that a couple of delicious cupcakes would be a nice treat for Wyatt."

"I suppose that someday you'll actually get that date with him," said Meadow. "Although at this point I think you're jinxed. Maybe you need to stop making plans and bodies will stop popping up."

"Well, technically, we did manage to have our picnic," said Beatrice.

"Yes, but it was cut tragically short. It wasn't as if you were able to get through the *entire* date. I don't think we can count a mere picnic as a full date," said Meadow decidedly.

Georgia and Savannah beamed at them as they sat down with them at the café table. "It's so good to see you both!" said Georgia in a bubbly way. "Savannah and I were just talking about quilting and then two of our guild members walked in."

"What were you talking about?" asked Beatrice.

Georgia laughed. "I was sitting here absolutely amazed that Savannah had kind words to say about the mystery quilt that Posy is sending out to us."

Beatrice winced a little. She hadn't been working on the quilt lately and had some catch-up work to do. So she couldn't exactly comment on the technicalities of the quilt.

Meadow, probably in an effort to stay extremely busy while waiting for Ash's proposal, apparently *had* been working on the quilt. "Oh, I bet I know what you're going to say, Savannah. You're actually working on a quilt that *isn't* full of geometric patterns and shapes. And ... do my ears deceive me? You actually *like* it?"

Savannah gave a long-suffering sigh, but her eyes danced a little. "I wouldn't say that I want to work on a quilt like this *all* the time, but, yes, I've actually liked it a little."

"Maybe that's because you're trying something different," suggested Beatrice.

"That's right. If you create the same thing all the time, even something that you love, you've got to get tired of doing it after a while," said Georgia.

Beatrice absently wiped a cupcake crumb off the corner of her mouth. "And just think—when you try something new, you never know what might happen as a result. Take June Bug, for instance. We know she loves quilting and baking. But she was running herself ragged doing the same thing all the time and not really thinking out of the box."

"She sure was!" Savannah made a face. "I have never seen her where she wasn't galloping off to deliver a cake or clean someone's house. Or both."

"Now she's probably just as busy, but she's at least in one spot. Not just that, but she's in a shop that she owns and has some control over. And she's not having to clean houses, which was just adding to her already-crazy schedule and making her exhausted," said Beatrice. "All because she was willing to try something new."

Georgia nodded. "That's how I ended up making pet clothes. And you know how much fun I have doing that."

Savannah said good-naturedly, "All right, all right. I've got the point. But remember—I didn't say I wanted to try something new all the time. It's just temporary. Now let's talk about something else. Any news, Meadow and Beatrice?"

Her words had the unfortunate effect of making Meadow turn bright red. Keeping Piper and Ash's possibly-pending engagement quiet was apparently killing Meadow. Beatrice sighed. Meadow really couldn't keep a secret to save her life. She decided to step in.

"We've been trying to find out information about poor Minerva's death, haven't we, Meadow?" prompted Beatrice.

Meadow, still very flustered but willing to grab the floatation device, quickly said, "Oh yes, yes. We've been asking some questions around."

"I've felt so awful about Minerva. From what I heard ... was there someone lying in wait for her at the park?" asked Georgia anxiously.

"The park has always felt like such a safe place. I'd hate to think that there are people hiding out there to attack other people," said Savannah in a severe voice. She carefully stacked Georgia's and her empty plates and put them in the corner of the table.

Beatrice said, "I don't think you have anything to worry about. From what I've been able to tell, this was something specific to Minerva. She was the one who had the routine that she followed there."

"Those poor birds!" said Georgia. "Who's going to fill their feeders now?"

Meadow waved her hand. "There's a whole group of volunteers that take turns filling the feeders at the park. But I guess the group will have to fill the gap, for sure. What we were more worried about was putting whoever did this behind bars. For good! Because we all want to feel completely safe again in Dappled Hills."

"Ramsay is on the job," said Savannah. "I'm sure the bad guy will be caught in no time."

"I wish I were that sure!" said Meadow. She peeled the paper off her second cupcake. "That's why Beatrice and I are trying to help him out. You know Beatrice has a knack for this sort of thing."

Georgia smiled. "You're a regular private eye, Beatrice. I'm glad you're on the case."

Beatrice said, "Well, I don't know about that. I think that mostly I just nose around a lot. And you could help us out, actually. Did either of you go near the park yesterday morning? Have you seen anything unusual?"

Savannah said, "I was at home with Smoke, sleeping in. Every once in a while it's nice to ignore the clock and curl up in bed with a cat. But Georgia, didn't you have to go out yesterday morning?"

"I did. I went grocery shopping really early because we were out of milk and eggs," said Georgia.

Savannah and Georgia usually biked everywhere in Dappled Hills instead of driving. It was amazing what they could manage while biking at the same time. But still. Beatrice asked, "You didn't bike home with *eggs*, did you?"

Georgia laughed. "Well, of course I did! Eggs are easy because you just thread the bag through your handlebar. The milk was a little trickier because it's so heavy. I carried it in a backpack on my back. And I went right by the park."

Meadow said, "Well, spill it! Who did you see?"

"I did see Minerva getting ready to go in. She was unpacking a lot of birdseed from her car. I rang the bike bell at her and she waved to me." Now Georgia looked more sober. "I guess I was the last person to see her alive. Oh, wait. No, probably not. Because I saw that Hazel was walking up to the parking lot."

"Hazel?" chorused Beatrice and Meadow.

"That's right. She looked as if she'd taken her dog for a walk. She has that little Chihuahua," said Georgia.

Savannah snorted and murmured, "I think Smoke is bigger than that dog."

"Hazel was there? That's interesting," said Beatrice. "Thanks, Georgia."

They finished eating and left at the same time as Georgia and Savannah.

As Meadow and Beatrice got in the car, Meadow said darkly, "So, it's Hazel. Hazel! Of all people. She was tricking us all the time. We thought she was simply Hazel the Happy Quilter and instead she was lying in wait for Minerva with malice in her heart. Wait until I tell Ramsay!"

"Meadow, we can't jump to conclusions. Just because Hazel was there walking her dog on a nice day doesn't necessarily mean that she is the guilty party. After all, think about it—would *you* want to try to kill someone with your dog right there? How would you sneak up on someone to kill them with those little dog toenails clicking from a mile away? And her dog probably would be barking too when he spotted Minerva. There's no way you'd have the element of surprise. And Minerva struck me as the kind of person you'd want to surprise if you were going to try to hit them over the head with a wrench."

Meadow seemed somewhat less upset. "Well, okay. Maybe it wasn't Hazel. But she still could have put her dog in the car and *then* gone back to sneak up on Minerva. Besides, Minerva could get so absorbed in what she was doing that I'm not so sure she would have been listening for little noises. The outdoors *is* noisy. There are birds and squirrels chattering and deer careening through the woods. I've seen Minerva totally focused on quilting, and she was so into it that I think a bus could have smashed into the shop and she wouldn't have noticed."

"And that's something to consider. But we still don't have enough evidence against Hazel to be sure that it's her," said Beatrice.

"I wonder if Hazel just *really* didn't want the whole town to know that she steals things," said Meadow. "I don't think the people of Dappled Hills would be happy to hear it. And they'd never look at her the same way. That's one thing about people in small towns—they never forget." She sighed. "So where to now? I'm still wanting to kill time and I don't think I can stand it being at home by myself. Ramsay's out investigating with Lieutenant Thomas and the SBI and I'd be alone and waiting for news from Ash."

Beatrice had planned on spending a quiet afternoon and evening at home. Then, maybe, have a small celebration if Piper rang with exciting news. But she could tell that Meadow was way too worked up to go back home.

"Why don't you come back with me?" asked Beatrice. "Maybe we can even get some quilting done. I'm a little behind on the mystery quilt and could probably stand to work on another project, too."

Meadow beamed at her. "What a great idea! Except ... well, can I bring Boris with me? I hate the idea of the poor thing being left alone over there and he'll probably need to go tinkle while I'm gone."

This definitely made it sound as if Meadow were planning on staying for the long run at Beatrice's. Beatrice forced a smile. "Of course!"

Meadow stopped by her house and picked up a quilt in progress and Boris, who was beside himself with excitement to get in the car.

"We go on lots of walks, but not as many rides in the car," explained Meadow with a laugh. "Okay if we put the windows down? It's such a short ride and I want him to enjoy every second."

With that, Boris stuck half of his tremendous body out the window to sniff the air on the way. He wriggled with joy. Beatrice wondered how Meadow was able to see out the windshield to drive the car. She was ready to evacuate at a moment's notice since Meadow was driving slow enough to safely do so.

They made it back home and it ended up being a much more entertaining visit than Beatrice had thought.

First, Meadow surveyed everything in Beatrice's fridge and pantry and said, "I know we recently ate cupcakes, but I swear I'm starving again. Maybe it's the excitement. How about if I whip up a meal with what you've got here in your house?"

Beatrice couldn't conceive how the odds and ends that she had in her house could possibly qualify for a meal, but she was very curious to see what Meadow would do with them. "Sounds good. I should be able to eat again, soon."

Somehow, Meadow ended up making some sort of spaghetti frittata with leftover pasta, eggs, milk, and a bunch of vegetables. Beatrice stared in wonder as Meadow fried it up in a pan. "Meadow, I don't even know how you figured that out."

"It's easy!" said Meadow blithely. "Didn't you ever really cook before?"

"I did, but it was long ago. And I think it involved a slow cooker most of the time," said Beatrice.

Boris and Noo-noo watched with great interest as Beatrice attempted to corral her spaghetti. Unluckily for them, she was able to eat up every bite. And she felt as if she were eating somewhat healthily too, carbs aside.

Meadow attacked her own plate with gusto. Afterward, Beatrice pulled out the wine. "A celebratory glass?" asked Meadow happily.

Beatrice still wanted to be cautious. She *knew* Piper loved Ash, but what if she wanted to wait a while longer before marrying? So instead she said, "How about a glass to celebrate the day? A good day with friends."

"I'll drink to that!" said Meadow.

They pulled out their quilts and worked on them for a while. Noo-noo and Boris, fortified by a few treats, took a nap nearby. It was mostly quiet, with Meadow humming an old tune every now and then, which was punctuated by the snores from the two dogs and the sewing machine as Beatrice finished some stitching. Meadow was working by hand with a quilting hoop.

There was a knock on the door about an hour into their quilting. Beatrice looked up, surprised, and still in her own little quilting world. But Meadow, apparently still on edge, leaped up from the sofa and galloped over to the front door. "Oh! Oh!" she breathed as she ran.

Meadow yanked open the door as a bleary-eyed Boris and Noo-noo struggled to their feet. Boris gave a half-hearted bark.

It was Piper and Ash, arm in arm and smiling from ear to ear.

Chapter Fourteen

"Imagine seeing the two of you together!" said Ash with a wink at Beatrice. "Mama was too wound up to be alone?"

"A little," laughed Beatrice a bit breathlessly.

Meadow fussed, "For heaven's sake! Tell us! What happened?"

Piper rather shyly reached out her left arm to show a lovely engagement ring on her finger. The ring was clearly vintage with a European cut diamond and filigree details in a white-gold Edwardian style.

Meadow immediately teared up. "My dear grandmother's ring. And it's so beautiful on your finger. Oh, Piper!"

And it ended up being good that Ash still had his arm around Piper because otherwise, the force of Meadow's hug might have made Piper stumble.

Then it was Beatrice's turn to hug them both and then it was just hugs all round. Then there really *was* a celebratory glass of wine.

Beatrice found a wedge of Brie cheese in her fridge and an unopened box of crackers and they all had a snack and chatted happily.

Meadow said to Piper, "And isn't it good to know that your mother *isn't* losing her mind?"

Piper smiled back at her. "Do you mean her odd desire to paint her living room after she swore she'd never paint again?"

"I do keep a list of local painters handy," said Beatrice, nodding.

"Or do you mean her equally odd desire to try a quilt with 'poetry' on it?" asked Piper.

Meadow said, "Well, who'd have thought you'd have such grim taste in poetry?"

"That's what I'm still shaking my head over," said Ash with a laugh. "What was it—'The Wasteland,' or something—as your favorite poem?"

"No, no, it was Edgar Allan Poe's poem. Of all things!" said Meadow.

"And 'The Lady of Shalott,'" added Piper.

"Hardly any better, from what I remember from high school English. Not exactly the most cheerful poetry in the world," said Ash.

Piper poked him teasingly. "I probably could have made a more suitable selection if I'd known it was for a proposal quilt. But it couldn't have made the quilt better in any way. I love it exactly the way it is. When I think of Ash coming up with such a meaningful way to propose and then Mama and Meadow working so hard on it." She choked up and stopped talking.

Meadow immediately choked up too and Beatrice quickly intervened, fearing that she'd have to go searching in her closets for tissue boxes. "And you forgot the biggest sacrifice," she added with a smile. "The fact that Meadow kept a secret for so long!"

They laughed and Meadow's tears thankfully dried quickly. "You're right, Beatrice! That was the hardest thing of all. I must have bitten my tongue about a hundred times since Ash first told me about it. And then Posy kept asking me what quilt I was currently working on and I couldn't really *say* what I was working on."

"Your face turned a real rainbow of colors when you were trying not to spill the beans," said Beatrice, grinning at the memory. "One thing can be said about you—you're fond of telling the truth!"

"And my discomfort was worth every minute! Now we know that I really *can* keep a secret, under duress. I'm just so, so happy for both of you," said Meadow, tears glistening once again in her eyes.

The good evening and happiness extended that night into Beatrice's dreams and she woke with a smile on her face.

The next couple of days flew by in a happy blur. Beatrice offered to help Piper with another round of grading and took care of it while Piper was at school. In the late afternoons when she was back home, Piper and Beatrice discussed flowers, dresses, colors, and food for the wedding. Meadow, surprisingly, didn't try to insert herself into the process, although she was thrilled when Piper called her to ask her opinion on incorporating quilting into the wedding.

Wyatt, Posy, Savannah, Georgia, and June Bug all called or ran by to give Beatrice a hug and to talk about Mother of the Bride dresses. Well, Wyatt didn't discuss dresses, but was supportive and excited for her.

Georgia was more than just supportive and excited. "I'm happy to have someone to bounce wedding ideas off of! I feel like it's such a boring subject for most people—but Piper and I can share tips!"

Finally, by the middle of the week, Beatrice was ready to get back into some sort of a routine. There hadn't been any news from the case except for Ramsay quietly confirming that it was indeed blunt force trauma that killed Minerva and that her funeral service was expected on Thursday.

Beatrice decided to make two phone calls. One to Wyatt, first of all.

"Everything going well with the planning?" he asked.

"Oh, I think we have plenty of time to plan. At first it's just so exciting and you brainstorm and come up with so many ideas. And then it's just sort of exhausting, calling the different places and researching ideas online. I thought that what I'd like most right now is for you and me to schedule our dinner together."

Wyatt's voice was pleased on the other side of the line. "I'd love that."

"Would tonight be good?" asked Beatrice.

Wyatt said, "It could work, but I'd rather plan for tomorrow night. I've got two pastoral visit plans for late afternoon and there's a good chance that one or more of them will run late. How is tomorrow for you?"

"It's fine for me, but are you sure it's good for you? What time is Minerva's service?" asked Beatrice.

Wyatt said, "Her service is at eleven in the morning. I have a feeling the funeral may run a bit over, but even if it does, I'll be completely free by the evening. Where would you like to go out to eat?"

"You know, it will have been a busy day. How about if I cook for you at my house?" asked Beatrice.

"Oh, I hate to have you go to the trouble," said Wyatt quickly.

"No, really, it's long overdue. You've cooked for me many times and I rarely return the favor."

Wyatt said, "In that case, I'd love it. What time?"

"Let's shoot for six," said Beatrice.

And she crossed her fingers that this time their meal would actually happen.

The next morning, Meadow called her around breakfast.

"Would you like a ride to Minerva's service?" she asked.

Beatrice said, "Actually, I think I'm going there directly after running an errand, so I won't need a ride."

"You're being rather mysterious. Does this errand have anything to do with the case?" demanded Meadow. "I thought I was your trusty sidekick!"

"It does. I'm going to the library to check out Orrilla's alibi. But think about it, Meadow—if we both show up there and start harassing the librarian in a public place about an alibi, we're going to really draw attention to ourselves. I don't think both of us need to be there."

Meadow sounded somewhat appeased. "Well, all right. I guess it's not as if both of us should check that out. But if you're going to question any of our suspects, make sure I'm with you. It's getting dangerous."

"I'm sure there will be some folks at the funeral that we can talk to. I'll look for you there," said Beatrice. She glanced at her watch. If she were going to the funeral directly after the library visit, she needed to find her most somber outfit and get dressed right away.

Thirty minutes later, she was parking at the library. It was the kind of library you might find in a storybook—a brick building with black shutters and ivy growing up along the front and sides. A very elderly groundskeeper was tending to the rose bushes in the front. He nodded to Beatrice as she approached. He'd seen Beatrice there just last week, picking up a novel and a biography. Along with what Ramsay had given her, she was now effectively swamped with reading material.

She climbed the concrete stairs outside and pushed open one of the glass doors into the building. Although it was still early in the day, the library was buzzing. There appeared to be a preschool storytelling hour going on in the juvenile section and Beatrice could hear the kids' laughter spilling out from the small room. There were some older men sitting comfortably in chairs by the fireplace reading magazines and looking sleepy. And there were several people on computers in the area toward the back.

Beatrice glanced over at the circulation desk and recognized one of the librarians there as someone who worked most days. She had black hair streaked with white and red glasses that matched Meadow's. She was also very observant. She noticed Beatrice quizzically looking her way and smiled at her.

"Can I help you?" she called.

Since there was no one at circulation, Beatrice decided that it was a good time to ask her a few questions. "Hi, I'm Beatrice Coleman."

The librarian nodded. "I remember you from all the times you've checked out. How is that book on Teddy Roosevelt?"

Beatrice raised her eyebrows. Here was someone who seemed blessed with an extraordinarily good memory. "To be honest, I haven't had a chance to start it yet. A friend of mine gave me a book to read, plus some short stories, so I took a break. But I do like the book so far."

The librarian said, "Of course, you're probably too busy to do much reading. You're one of the quilters, aren't you? I know we hosted some of your quilts when there have been shows in our community room, haven't we?" Seeing Beatrice's surprised look, she continued, "Oh, I always take note when one of our patrons is participating in the arts community. And I've always admired the quilts. I'm not crafty, but I enjoy seeing them."

"Yes, I'm one of the Village Quilters, although I wasn't a quilter until I moved here. Before then, though, I was involved in the arts community in Atlanta as a curator for a folk art museum there."

Beatrice chatted with the librarian about quilting for another minute or two, glancing up from time to time to ensure another library patron wasn't going to come up and interrupt them. Finally, she said, "Actually, I had something I wanted to ask you. It may seem an odd question, but did you happen to see Orrilla Bush here last Saturday morning?"

The librarian said, "She's one of the Cut-Ups, I believe. No, she was not here on Saturday. As I've already mentioned to the Chief of Police," she added gently.

Ramsay had definitely been on the trail. Beatrice blinked at the librarian. "You sound very sure about that. You couldn't have missed her?"

"No. That's because last Saturday morning we were closed. I should say that we opened late that day. Our heating and air conditioning system needed some work and the repair company asked us to give them some space. We opened at two p.m."

Beatrice said slowly, "I see. That's very interesting. Thank you."

"Of course, we do see some of your fellow quilters here, a couple more frequently than others," said the librarian, still trying to be helpful. "The poor woman who died recently, for instance. I saw her here nearly daily."

"Who is that?" asked Beatrice. "Do you mean Minerva Lundy?"

"Goodness, I'd forgotten. There were *two* recent deaths of quilters, weren't there? No, I meant the other woman—Henrietta. She came very frequently, although I didn't see very much of her about a month before her death. That's why I'd originally assumed she'd been ill before she died ... because I hadn't seen her at the library," said the librarian.

Beatrice frowned. She wouldn't have said that Henrietta struck her as a tremendous reader. "Henrietta was here daily reading magazines and newspapers? Checking out books?"

"No, I didn't get the impression she enjoyed reading for pleasure. She was here on the computer. It wasn't that she spent a *long* time here, but she was here very regularly and always gone in about fifteen or twenty minutes," said the librarian. She looked behind Beatrice, smiling at someone else. "And now, I'm sorry, but I need to check a patron's books out. Hope you enjoy that Roosevelt book."

Beatrice absently thanked her and walked back toward the door. That was odd, wasn't it? Henrietta certainly had her own computer—she'd seen it herself when she'd found her body. Why would she be taking the time and trouble to use the library's?

As Beatrice walked outside, she nearly ran into Julia. Julia raised her eyebrows at Beatrice's empty arms. "Returning a book?" she asked in something of a sarcastic voice.

"Oh, I've got enough to read right now," said Beatrice. "Ramsay has given me a bunch of short stories and a book to read, so I'm in good shape."

"And you and Ramsay are great friends, apparently?" asked Julia sharply.

"Well, certainly. I'm over there all the time, after all," said Beatrice, frowning. She couldn't quite understand what Julia was getting at.

"At least you're open about it," said Julia with a short laugh.

"Open about what? Visiting Meadow and Ramsay and Boris the dog? Why shouldn't I be? There's nothing scurrilous about it, so just disabuse yourself of that notion." Now Beatrice was getting steamed up. She hadn't quite gotten used to the gossipy aspect in some small towns. Particularly when there was nothing to gossip about.

"Whatever you say," said Julia in a condescending voice. "Maybe it's something very different. Maybe you're an apprentice trying to learn the sleuthing biz. You sure ask a lot of nosy questions."

"Which reminds me—while I've got you," said Beatrice, feeling her claws coming out, "where were you when Minerva was murdered? Don't you spend a good deal of time at the park?"

"Doesn't *everyone* spend a good deal of time at the park?" asked Julia. She studied her fingernail polish with bored eyes. "It's not as if there's very much to do here. One must take advantage of all of the amenities."

"But on Saturday? Were you there on Saturday?" asked Beatrice.

"As it happens, no, I wasn't there on Saturday. I was catching up on my sleep that morning. I haven't been able to sleep soundly for a while now and I finally took a little something to knock me out on Friday night. I was finally waking up around eleven o'clock," said Julia.

Beatrice raised her eyebrows. "Has something tired you out lately?"

"Lack of sleep, as I said. You may not know, but I have a very successful blog. I'm passionate about it, but it's draining. I'm always dealing with people interested in sponsoring it, people who want to guest post for it. And *I'm* always brainstorming new posts. It's a very time-consuming and tiring process," said Julia.

"What's your blog's theme? Gardening? Food?"

"Marriage. How to sustain your marriage and have a happy one," said Julia.

"And you and Jim have a happy marriage?" asked Beatrice.

Julia's eyebrows drew together fiercely, "Of course we do. Everyone says we're one of the happiest couples in Dappled Hills."

This was interesting, because Beatrice had never met Jim in all the times that she'd seen Julia. Their happy marriage apparently didn't depend on their spending much time together.

And her happiness didn't seem to gel with the fact that she was reported looking glazed. If it wasn't dementia, and Beatrice had seen no evidence in their conversation to support dementia, then could it be alcohol or drugs? And why would such a happy person be relying on those things?

"I've heard folks say," said Beatrice carefully, "that they've observed you looking very glassy-eyed and somewhat out-of-it lately. In fact, it was suggested that you might have dementia."

Julia looked surprised by this and gave another short laugh. "Small towns."

"Aside from forgetting to fill up your car with gasoline, I don't see that you're forgetful or have symptoms of dementia. So I'm wondering—are you struggling with addiction?" asked Beatrice.

Julia flushed and opened her mouth, likely to defensively snap at Beatrice. Then she closed her mouth abruptly. A few moments later, she said with some dignity, "As a matter of fact, you're right. I had a nasty car accident a couple of years ago and it took time to recover from it. The doctor tried to manage my pain with painkillers, but apparently I've got an addictive personality. I started seeing several different doctors and they all prescribed painkillers. I got hooked." She opened her hands helplessly.

"Is that what Henrietta found out and blackmailed you over? Because being addicted to painkillers after being genuinely prescribed them is something of an epidemic, isn't it?" asked Beatrice.

"Henrietta thought of it more as a personal failing," said Julia sourly. "I did pay her for a while, but more recently I've just tried to get myself off of the painkillers instead of paying to cover the problem up. It's been very hard."

A humble Julia was a lot more sympathetic figure. Beatrice said, "I can imagine how hard that would be. Good for you for doing it."

Changing the subject slightly, Beatrice added, "And speaking of Henrietta, I just learned that she spent a good deal of time here at the library. On the computer, apparently. Would you have any ideas why she would do something like that?"

Julia's eyes became hooded and she abruptly shook her head. "Surprising, but I don't know anything about that. And now, I've really got to go. I need to pick up my book before the funeral."

Beatrice glanced at her watch. If she were going to make it to the funeral, she needed to get going, too.

Chapter Fifteen

A brisk wind was creating some havoc at the cemetery when Beatrice arrived. The funeral home representatives were casting concerned eyes at the tent covering the family. The funeral appeared to be everything that Henrietta's wasn't. For one thing, it appeared that most members of Minerva's family and her husband's family were there. There must have been fifty cousins, aunts, uncles, and other assorted relatives gathered. Aside from that, many people from Dappled Hills were there, too. She saw that Orrilla was there with her husband, Ted. Julia appeared to be attending by herself.

Beatrice could quickly tell that it wasn't going to be a short service, either. According to the program, there were quite a few speakers, soloists, and a sermon of some sort. She decided that she should have worn more comfortable shoes because she was going to be standing for a while.

Wyatt was speaking quietly to the family. At one point he made eye contact with Beatrice and gave her a quick smile.

Meadow spotted her from across the crowd of people and gave her a short wave and a helpless shrug to indicate that she wasn't sure she could get over to Beatrice any time soon. That was either due to the crowd or the fact that both Miss Sissy and Savannah appeared to be trying to have a conversation with her.

And right then, the service started and everyone stayed right in their spots for more than an hour.

At the end of the service, Beatrice was looking around for a bench to sit on when she was startled by a voice at her elbow. It was Hazel and she was looking fairly winded.

"Tired out? Me too. Longest service ever! Let's find a bench—I'll sit with you. Look! There's one over there that no one has discovered yet." Hazel grabbed her by the arm and fairly dragged her some yards away from the gathered mourners to a shady area where there was indeed a bench.

Beatrice could see that Meadow had finally broken away from chatty quilters and was walking with determination toward the bench, not wanting to be left out of any suspect questioning.

"Is there room for a third?" asked Meadow sweetly.

Beatrice sighed. On this particular bench, there really wasn't room for anyone else, other than perhaps a small child under the age of five. But there was no stopping Meadow. She slid over as far as she could.

Hazel said in a jolly voice, "Always room for a friend, Meadow! And that was a pretty long time to be standing, wasn't it? Although Minerva would have loved the service, I think—the family planned it perfectly. May she rest in peace."

Meadow said, "Tragic! So tragic! The Cut-Ups have lost *two* talented members."

"And I'm sure the recruiting for new guild members will happen after a decent amount of time has passed. But we'll need enough members to be able to do our community work and the quilt shows we do as a guild and that type of thing." Hazel paused and then looked over at Meadow with a bit of sadness in her eyes. "I suppose I'll be speaking to your hubby again soon. Nice man, of course. I just wish he weren't the bloodhound on the trail when he's around me."

Meadow's eyes opened wide. "Ramsay? A bloodhound? Are you sure you haven't mistaken him for some errant member of the state police that's here in town? Lieutenant Thomas, for instance?"

"I get the impression that the *last* thing Ramsay wants to do is investigate," agreed Beatrice. "I think he simply gets leads that he must follow up on. Which reminds me, Hazel: I did want to ask you one thing. Someone saw you in the park on Saturday morning—walking your dog."

Hazel's eyes opened wide. "Who on earth was that? I didn't see *anyone* when I was there." She stopped short in consternation, realizing that she'd confessed to being there. "Okay, yes, I was at the park. But I was only there for a walk. I didn't say anything about it because the *last* thing that I want to do is to draw more attention to myself or make Ramsay suspect me more."

Meadow jumped in, soothingly. "Of *course* you didn't! And walking a dog early in the morning makes perfect sense. Ramsay would certainly understand, Hazel."

Hazel seemed in the mood to confess all. Maybe it was the influence of the long service she'd just attended. Or maybe it was the fact that she had accidentally started confessing and she decided to keep going. "Well, you'd be very impressed seeing Ramsay in action, I promise you. You see, he's talked to a lot of different people in town. That's probably what makes him such a good cop. He visits with people and people tell him things. They trust him. And he grew up in Dappled Hills so it's not like folks don't know him. He talked to enough people to realize that perhaps, *perhaps*, I have a slight problem with ... er, general, low-level thievery." She blushed slightly.

Beatrice quickly inserted before Meadow could give Hazel a bunch of reassurances, "Meadow and I actually heard just a slight inkling about that, too."

"Not a *lot*," said Meadow stoutly. "It's not as if the whole town was talking about it."

"That's right. Just a hint," said Beatrice in a soothing way.

Hazel said sadly, "At this point, I don't know if it matters. I think I'm tired of my life of crime and I'm ready to own up to it. But I didn't have anything to do with what happened in the park, I promise you. No, my secrets are pretty minor stuff. And secrets in a small town are just too hard to keep. It's very, very stressful. Now I'll just face the consequences."

"I'm not at all sure there would be consequences to face," protested Meadow. "It seems to me that these people that snitched on you to Ramsay would have to press charges or something. And I haven't heard anything about that. Or anything about you possibly being arrested. Ramsay would surely tell me if that were the case, believe me."

Her voice suggested that Ramsay had better.

Beatrice said slowly, "But I think Hazel might be talking about other consequences, not just jail time. The consequences of everyone knowing what you've done."

"Exactly," said Hazel, beaming at Beatrice as if she were a prize student. "That's exactly right. I'd hate to walk through town and see people subconsciously pull their purses closer to them or check their pockets for their cell phones. It would be really awful."

"So what are you planning on doing?" demanded Meadow. Her face showed that she suspected what Hazel's answer was going to be.

"Moving," said Hazel, holding out her hands.

"Moving! But what about the Cut-Ups?"

Naturally, that would be Meadow's first thought.

Hazel looked at her with sad eyes. "Meadow, much as I love quilting and I love that feeling of being part of a group, you've got to know that the Cut-Ups isn't quite as close a guild as the Village Quilters. I'm sure they'll be able to find someone else to take my place."

"You could join in the Village Quilters! We'd be happy to take you in and no one judges anyone else in the group. We all have our issues there—having another member with issues wouldn't be a problem at all!" Meadow was enthusiastically waving her hands around and threatening to fall off the bench at the same time.

Beatrice said, "Meadow, it sounds as if Hazel may have a plan of some kind. Let's hear what her plan is, first."

Hazel gave her a grateful glance. "As a matter of fact, I do. My daughter lives in Charlotte with my grandbaby and she's in a guild there. I've always thought it would be a fun place to live, but I didn't want to horn in on her family. But she said that she might need a hand around the house. And they have plenty of room for one more. I get along well with her husband, too. So, in a way, this is what I needed to get myself organized and ready to move. I'll be back for visits. Sometimes you just need to make a change. And I, for sure, needed to make one."

Beatrice asked, "The things you took? Was it just some sort of compulsion that drove you to do it?"

"Because you don't seem the sort!" said Meadow.

"No, no compulsion. No medical reason to do it," said Hazel cheerfully. "Just the fact that I desperately needed money. I have the feeling that neither of you know what that's really like. Maybe you thought I just *liked* wearing the same thing three days out of the week or that I walked places instead of taking my car so that I could get some exercise. If you saw my pantry and fridge, you'd see that there are slim-pickings in there. So I'd take a little something, when it was easy to do it. I wasn't breaking or entering or anything. I'd just grab little things here and there and then sell them online. The people I took from probably thought they'd misplaced their stuff and they ended up replacing it. I knew it wasn't the right thing to do. And I know I *should* be paying for it. But I think I'll just head out of town. After Ramsay gives me the all-clear," she added with a laugh. "The last thing I need is to be a fugitive on top of everything else. I don't think he'd want one of his suspects leaving town."

Beatrice said, "And you're a suspect because Henrietta found out, didn't she? She knew that you had been stealing things."

Hazel nodded. "Came right into my house and spotted something that belonged to another one of the Cut-Ups."

Meadow gasped at the idea of quilters stealing from each other and Hazel said sadly, "It wasn't right, was it?"

"So Henrietta saw something and confronted you about it?" asked Beatrice.

"Not at all. She took a picture of the thing ... I think it was a phone ... and then she sent me a letter the next day. Asking for money to keep quiet. The only problem was that I didn't have a lot of money to pay out." For the first time, Hazel's eyes glittered with anger. Henrietta's blackmail had made her furious, that much was obvious.

But the anger was gone as quickly as it had arrived. Hazel said with her usual sunny smile, "Well, I guess I've rested here long enough. Let me give my condolences to the family and then I'll be on my way. Good seeing you girls."

Beatrice and Meadow watched as Hazel walked off to the family.

"So ... Hazel! I didn't ever *really* suspect her, but she sure does seem like someone who could have killed Henrietta. Did you see how mad she got, just thinking about how Henrietta had blackmailed her? She really *could* have killed her in a fit of anger," said Meadow.

Beatrice said, still watching Hazel talk animatedly with Minerva's family, "She definitely had motive, no question about it."

"I wish I'd known that she was going through hard times. I'd have helped her!" said Meadow, shaking her head. "I can't believe that I didn't know about it—I'm really going to beat myself up over that. The idea that she was suffering enough to start stealing from her friends and other quilters! It's hard to wrap my head around, it really is."

Beatrice said, "I guess she was too ashamed to ask for help and have everyone in town know about her need."

"I wish she had, though. I wouldn't have told anyone, but I could definitely have helped out with the food. I'd have brought her a basket every other day," said Meadow in a determined voice.

Meadow would have, too. Especially with the huge amount of baking and cooking she did every single day.

Meadow sighed. "Well, onto other topics, since this one is making me sad. What did you find out at the library?"

Beatrice's eyes slid over to where Orrilla was talking to one of Minerva's family. "I found out that Orrilla was certainly not at the library on Saturday morning when she says that she was."

"No!" Meadow's eyes were wide. "How brazen of her to tell us that she was!"

"I think she thought she could get away with it. After all, she must have figured the librarian couldn't possibly note when every single person goes in and out of the library. Maybe the librarian could be busy checking out books or shelving magazines or something. But in this case, she was wrong. The library was actually closed for repairs on Saturday morning."

If possible, Meadow's eyes grew even wider.

"But the librarian said that she was used to seeing quilters at the library—in particular, Henrietta," said Beatrice.

Meadow frowned. "I don't think I ever had a conversation with Henrietta about books in my life. Nor Ramsay, and he certainly would have if he thought she was a big reader."

"That's the thing—apparently, she wasn't reading there or checking out books. She was using the library's computers," said Beatrice.

"But she had her own computer. Why on earth would she wait for one at the public library?" asked Meadow.

"That's what I wondered. But I just had a thought—what if she were using the library's computer because she didn't want anyone to know who she was? What if Henrietta was the troll on Julia's blog?" asked Beatrice.

Meadow sighed. "Well, if you'd asked me about it a couple of months ago, I'd have said that was the craziest thing I'd ever heard. Now I've heard so much about Henrietta that I'd say that's just about par for the course. Why else *would* she do it? There's usually a line at the library of folks wanting to use their computers, so it wouldn't have been an *easy* thing to do. But why *would* she leave mean comments on Julia's blog? What would she gain?"

"As a matter of fact, I ran into Julia while I was there. She reinforced our belief that the blog was a major source of income. Julia also confirmed that she had a problem kicking painkillers that she was prescribed after an accident," said Beatrice.

Meadow nodded. "That's right, I remember the accident. People were saying she was lucky to be alive. I brought food over there for weeks."

"Maybe Henrietta found out about Julia's addiction and tried to blackmail her," said Beatrice slowly.

"But Julia didn't want to be blackmailed," asked Meadow. She waved as Julia and Orrilla left the cemetery together.

"Exactly. Julia may have acted like it wasn't that big of a deal. But Henrietta knew about Julia's blog and maybe she thought that if she left a bunch of nasty comments on it that Julia might feel pressure to pay up. After all, on the blog, Julia writes as if she has this perfect life," said Beatrice.

"Right. The only thing is that those comments on the blog didn't have to do with drugs or painkillers. They had to do with Julia's marriage." Meadow squinted across the cemetery and said, "Heavens! Miss Sissy! I was supposed to take her home." She scrambled to her feet.

"Where is she? I don't see her anywhere." Beatrice also stood up and felt a little stiff once she did.

"Surely someone would have told me if they took her home," fretted Meadow.

Beatrice said, "Wait a minute. The shade is casting a shadow there, but isn't that someone on that bench way on the other side of the cemetery?"

Meadow heaved a great sigh. "Thank goodness. That's Miss Sissy, for sure. Why didn't she come looking for me?"

The answer, as they walked over, was simple enough. Miss Sissy was sound asleep on the bench and snoring loudly. She awoke with a start and glared at Meadow and Beatrice as if they'd committed some heinous crime.

"Are you ready to go home, Miss Sissy?" asked Meadow sweetly. "I'm sorry it took me so long."

"Wickedness!" spat Miss Sissy, straightening her dress. Beatrice had been happy to note earlier that the old woman had decided to wear one of her usual dresses to the funeral instead of something inappropriate.

They got into Meadow's car and Beatrice said, "Well, it was a very nice service. I'm sure Minerva would have thought it was lovely and appropriate."

Miss Sissy muttered, "Wicked."

"Okay, Miss Sissy, you're going to have to explain yourself," said Beatrice gravely. "You know that there's someone very dangerous running around. If you know something that could help us find out who that person is, you've got to help us."

Miss Sissy gave her a sideways glance.

Beatrice prompted her. "When we were at Henrietta's funeral, you hissed at Minerva in passing. You didn't seem as if you liked her very much."

Miss Sissy squinted at her.

"Or, maybe, you seemed as though you didn't *approve* of her," amended Beatrice.

Meadow said, "That sounds more like it! Miss Sissy, what did Minerva do?"

The old woman mumbled, "Sorry she's dead."

"Of course. I'm sure Minerva didn't deserve to die. But she did *something*," pressed Beatrice.

"Another man. Not her husband," growled Miss Sissy.

Beatrice relaxed a little. Finally maybe they were getting somewhere. "Do you know who the man was? Where were they?"

"Saw them in the park when I was walking by. Wickedness!"

Chapter Sixteen

Beatrice feared Miss Sissy was about to get sidetracked by one of her rants. "Who was the man?"

"Don't know! But not her husband!" Miss Sissy gave Beatrice a resentful look for pushing the issue.

Meadow gave Beatrice an arched look. "We can mull over the possibilities later." She mouthed *when Miss Sissy isn't here.*

"We can, but not tonight!" said Beatrice quickly.

Meadow clapped her hands, making Miss Sissy scowl even more fiercely at her. "Wyatt? Finally? White tablecloth, to make up for all the previous trouble?"

"Wyatt, yes, but white tablecloth, no. We're having supper at my house," said Beatrice shortly. "After all our rescheduling and issues with trying to meet, I thought maybe we'd have a better chance of a date actually happening if we tried for it at my house." She sighed as Meadow looked more disapproving. "What's the problem with our plan, Meadow? I think my house will do fine for the cozy, romantic factor."

"Bah!" spat out Miss Sissy.

Meadow said, "Well, of *course* it will. Your house is the coziest, sweetest cottage around. It's the kind of place where you walk in and feel at home. You could even set up a little table for two in your backyard and enjoy all your impatiens and gardenias and rose bushes. But I was thinking about the *food*, Beatrice. What on earth are you going to do about the *food*? Because that's an important aspect of dinner, too."

As a matter of fact, and with a rising sense of panic, Beatrice realized that she hadn't actually considered the food at all. Oh, she'd planned on keeping it simple. And, in her mind, she thought she had it all under control.

Meadow was still talking as Beatrice was coming to this realization. "And this service took a while, didn't it? So now you need to plan what you want to eat, get the food, and cook it. What have you got in your house right now?"

Beatrice frowned, trying to recollect the contents of her freezer and pantry. Everything had been such a blur lately, from the picnic to Piper and Ash's engagement, to Minerva's funeral, that she hadn't really been in meal-planning or grocery-shopping mode. When she'd been at home, she'd tried to keep as quiet as possible.

"I suspect I have enough to do 'breakfast for supper'," said Beatrice slowly. As Meadow's face grew more and more horrified, Beatrice continued, "I've got waffle mix ... no, scratch that. I've got frozen waffles. And I'm sure I've got two or three eggs, although I've been out of pepper for a while and I do like a peppered egg. Then I have some leftover ham, although frankly, it's probably ready to be tossed."

Miss Sissy barked, "Scrap it!"

"Scrap it?" asked Beatrice.

Meadow said, "I'm afraid Miss Sissy's right. Breakfast for supper is absolutely fine and one of my most favorite things to eat. It would be completely perfect *if* you've had a date every night the past couple of weeks with Wyatt. Or even half that amount of time. But for an evening where you're trying to make meaningful time together after tragedies have intervened? And he's had a very busy day, after all—Wyatt only just left with the family a few minutes ago. " She shook her head. "It's not going to work, Beatrice. It smacks of not really caring."

Beatrice *did* care. She just felt remarkably uninspired in terms of cooking right now.

Meadow, as usual, had a plan.

"How about—and it would be my honor and pleasure, Beatrice—if I were to cook an amazing feast for the two of you?" asked Meadow anxiously.

"Mmm," said Miss Sissy, looking very much as if she would like an invitation to the supper herself."

"Could I do that, Beatrice? You know how I love to cook. And I know how you don't!" said Meadow.

"You're right about that," said Beatrice ruefully. She paused. "But you're right about the importance of showing some kind of effort—showing that our time together is important to us. It may not seem that way to Wyatt after all the date shuffling that we've had to do, although he seems very understanding about all of it. I shouldn't have thought it was all right to put down frozen waffles and a meager amount of scrambled eggs. But I don't think it would show effort to allow my entire meal to be catered by you, Meadow, much as I appreciate the offer. No, I'll run home and grab my recipes, plan a shopping list, and then head to the store."

Meadow said earnestly, "But Beatrice—keep it simple. Simple food tastes just as good. And you're showing effort by cooking! You don't have to go crazy with the menu."

"I'm going to stretch myself a little, Meadow. Not a lot, but a little. It'll give me a chance to divert my creativity into a different venue. That's got to be a good thing, right?" asked Beatrice.

Miss Sissy grimaced and shook her head.

Beatrice went by the store, old recipe cards in her hands. She wished they'd been recipes of something she'd actually cooked before, but instead they were of recipes that she'd *planned* on cooking before. Looking over them, however, they certainly didn't seem to be very hard. But they did seem to have a lot of ingredients. She frowned at the cards. Beatrice thought she remembered that Wyatt had a fondness for pork chops. And this was a recipe for herbed pork chops with a raspberry sauce. She'd decided to serve some green beans and julienned carrots with them. They were certainly something that would show effort.

And it might be fun to cook again—she'd limited what she'd tried for such a long time.

It took much longer than she'd expected, trying to find where everything was in the store. And apparently, Bub's Grocery wasn't one for stocking gourmet ingredients. She sighed. Maybe she should have planned to head to Lenoir to go to a larger grocery store. Beatrice was able to find the thyme, but Bub's didn't seem to carry sage. She had no problem finding raspberry jam, but it was considerably harder finding white wine vinegar. And the butcher seemed appalled that Beatrice wanted boneless pork chops for the recipe. He shot her rather reproachful looks as he specially prepared her meat.

Her trip to the grocery store had also made her realize that she hadn't eaten for a while and was hungry. Usually, she tried not to go to the store hungry since it made her buy too much food. Today she decided to run by June Bug's shop to grab another one of those muffins to hold her off until dinner.

This time she'd managed to catch June Bug in a quiet time at the shop. The little woman's round face beamed at her as she came in. "Beatrice!"

"I was in the grocery store and realized I was starving," said Beatrice with a grin. "Could I have another of your delicious muffins?"

"You and I will *both* have a muffin," said June Bug, efficiently plating several muffins of different varieties. She trotted around the counter which meant that Beatrice could now see more of her than just the little woman's head behind the counter. She was wearing black pants, a sparkling white tee-shirt, white tennis shoes, and an apron that appeared to be covered with cartoonish June bugs.

"I love your apron!" said Beatrice, admiring the multi-colored June bugs having picnics, driving cars, and playing cards on June Bug's apron.

June Bug smiled and bobbed her head. "Meadow found it for me. She finds the cutest things." She set the muffins and two plates in front of them. "You picked a good time to come visit."

"Was it crazy here earlier?" asked Beatrice as she chose a muffin that appeared to have blueberries in it. She took a bite and closed her eyes briefly in enjoyment. Blueberry cheesecake.

June Bug bobbed her head again and reached for a cinnamon swirl muffin. "Business has been good. There was a rush of people all at once," said June Bug.

"You obviously filled a need with your bakery. There *was* a bakery here, that bakery closed, and now *your* bakery is here. The nice thing is that it was already an established location to have cakes and muffins," said Beatrice.

June Bug's eyes were huge as she said solemnly, "And I can't thank you and Meadow and Posy enough for all you've done to get me set up here. My friends."

June Bug got a little teary, which made Beatrice a little teary. Which made Beatrice want to hurry on before she grew *more* teary. She said gruffly, "You know we loved to do it, June Bug."

June Bug carefully split the third muffin with a knife and gave Beatrice half. "This is a new one, if you'd like to try it. Pumpkin spice."

Beatrice took a bite and nodded happily.

They sat for a moment in silence and then June Bug asked, "How is everything going with the murder investigations? I felt so sorry for both of those ladies. Such fine quilters, too!"

"I know. It really is a shame. Meadow and I have been poking around in it, which you know we usually do. And we've gotten some information in bits and pieces. I'm just not totally sure how all the bits and pieces add up," said Beatrice.

June Bug's round face crinkled in a frown. "What are some of your pieces? I'd like to be able to help you, if I could."

"Well, one of them came from Miss Sissy. She always seems to know a lot about what's going on, but can't ever seem to *relate* it.

Anyway, she saw Minerva with someone who 'wasn't her husband.'"

June Bug nodded violently. "Yes!"

Beatrice leaned forward in the café chair. "Do you know who the man was?"

June Bug flushed. "I didn't catch them doing anything *bad* together," she said slowly, "but they did come here. Separately, you know. They didn't come in *with* each other. But they were definitely together."

"Who?" asked Beatrice. June Bug was starting to sound like Miss Sissy.

"Minerva and Julia's husband." June Bug gave Beatrice an anxious look and glanced around them quickly as if a stray customer could somehow have slipped into the shop without her notice.

"Oh! Oh, I see. Jim is his name, isn't it?"

June Bug nodded again.

"I'll have to ask Miss Sissy if that's who she saw Minerva with. Maybe, if I describe him, then she can confirm it. Although I don't even really know what he looks like, myself, since he's so elusive," said Beatrice frowning.

"Dark hair, thin, lots of teeth," said June Bug helpfully. She trotted back behind the counter and came quickly back with two lemonades with red and white striped straws. "What other bits and pieces do you have?"

"Well, there's Hazel. She was apparently at the park the morning that Minerva died. And she was also trying to hide something that Henrietta knew about. But Hazel always seems so jolly and matter-of-fact that it's hard to think of her as someone who'd be angry or cold enough to murder." Beatrice took another bite of the blueberry cheesecake muffin and washed it down with her lemonade.

June Bug said in a low voice, her protruding eyes even larger, "She's nice. I like Hazel. But she gets mad sometimes, too. One day I was taking the trash out here and heard her get so mad at someone. It was that little alley behind the shop and I guess she thought she wouldn't run into anyone. Hazel was really yelling at them. Said that she couldn't take it anymore. I couldn't see who she was talking to."

Beatrice said thoughtfully, "I wonder if that could have been Henrietta. I know Hazel is worried that the whole town would know her secret and then it would be hard to live here. It's interesting to know that she *does* actually have a temper." She glanced at her watch and said ruefully, "And now, unfortunately, I've got to go. Thank you for being so helpful, June Bug. I've got all those groceries in the car and if I don't get home soon, dinner will be ruined before I've even had a chance to try to ruin it myself. How much do I owe you?"

June Bug shook her head, busily collecting the plates and glasses and trotting around the counter with them. "Not a penny. Not after all you've done for me."

Beatrice smiled at her. "I'll accept that sweet gesture as long as it's *this time only*. We'll call ourselves even. You've given me helpful information, after all."

"Even." June Bug gave her a shy smile and waved cheerily at her as Beatrice hurried out the door.

Beatrice meant to call Meadow and ask her for the white wine vinegar so that she could swing by before she went home. But she was distracted thinking about the meal she was about to cook. She went directly home and changed from her funeral clothes into some old khakis and a tired-looking button-down shirt. She'd have time to change again before Wyatt got there and she didn't much feel like wrangling the food while wearing her nice clothes.

She had the pork chops rubbed with the herbs by the time she remembered. Her hands were actually herb-covered too, and she had to wash up to get on the phone.

"Meadow? Do you happen to have any white wine vinegar?" asked Beatrice.

"White wine vinegar? Oh dear. Did you try one of those fancy recipes?" Meadow's voice was solicitous on the other end.

"It's fancy, but it's not hard," said Beatrice dismissively. "But Bub's wasn't exactly a great source for the ingredients. You cook so much that I figured you might have some around your kitchen somewhere."

"I certainly do. But I think you could probably just substitute with white wine, instead. Vinegar can so easily be overdone." The concern in Meadow's voice had definitely escalated.

The concern made Beatrice rather defensive as a result. Clearly, Meadow thought Beatrice could potentially ruin an entire meal by adding too much vinegar to it. But she did have white wine.

"I'll give the white wine a go, then. Thanks, Meadow."

"What is it you're cooking?" asked Meadow, still worried.

"Pork chops. Don't worry, it'll be easy. And I know Wyatt really likes pork chops, too," said Beatrice.

"Well, then, that sounds like a good pick," said Meadow in a deliberately cheerful tone. "Hope y'all enjoy a lovely dinner."

The thing was that Meadow wasn't entirely wrong. The dinner was a little tricky. She needed to do a couple of things nearly at once and she was much more of a linear cook, not a multi-tasking one. There was the pan-cooking of the pork chops on both sides. She soon discovered that her pans were not up to the job of cooking more than one pork chop at a time. Beatrice sighed and nearly called Meadow back to ask to borrow a larger frying pan. But then she decided she'd just make the pork chops in shifts and keep them warm in the oven while she was boiling the raspberry jam, orange juice, and the wine.

She was working on the second pork chop when there was a knock at the door. Beatrice frowned and squinted at the clock. Wyatt was a bit early, wasn't he? And she'd gotten so caught up in the cooking part of the evening that she wasn't even ready. She hadn't had a chance to change again into nicer clothes.

Beatrice grabbed a dish towel since her hands were splotched with food and hurried to the door.

And saw Julia standing there.

Chapter Seventeen

Suddenly, seeing Julia, even with a benign expression on her face, made everything very, very clear to Beatrice. The library and Henrietta. Miss Sissy's feelings toward Minerva. June Bug's story.

Beatrice, her heart pounding, tried to slam the door shut but Julia was too quick for her.

"I *thought* so," snarled Julia. "Nosy woman. I could tell that you'd figured something out." She took a large knife out of the purse she carried on her arm.

Beatrice heart pounded, but she said in a calm voice, "Julia, you're not making any sense. I'm sure you must have been seen here. Is your car parked outside?"

Julia shook her head with a smirk and took a step closer to Beatrice, who took a step back. Noo-noo, sensing the tension, started making low growling noises.

"I didn't drive here; I walked."

"Then someone would have seen you walking over, Julia. This is a very busy road. Ramsay himself drives up and down it a dozen times a day," said Beatrice, trying to keep calm.

"I didn't see a soul. If I had, I'd have just slipped into the woods until they passed. After all, we're neighbors, Beatrice. Not that you've ever been super-friendly," said Julia, sounding a bit peeved.

Beatrice almost gave a laugh. Was Julia just trying to make excuses for why she needed to get rid of Beatrice? Surely Beatrice, as the *new* neighbor, should have been the one receiving visits from Julia. She said, "I'm fairly quiet and don't do a lot of visiting, I'm afraid. And you were wrong. I didn't really know anything about your connection to the murders. Oh, I had my *suspicions*, but I hadn't really had any time to think about them—it's been that busy." She spared a thought for the pork chops, which were starting to create an acrid, burning smell.

But Julia didn't seem to notice the food smell or pay attention to Beatrice's protests. "What about this morning, when you were taunting me about Ramsay. I wasn't going to be blackmailed again, Beatrice. You shouldn't have thought I was going to go along that easily."

She pointed the knife at Beatrice as she spoke and Noo-noo started barking at Julia and looking up to Beatrice for any signals for how to act. But Beatrice kept her eyes trained on Julia. Then, when Julia started looking at Noo-noo, who was increasingly agitated, Beatrice glanced around for something she could use as a weapon against Julia. Her belongings appeared completely innocuous and unworthy as weapons of any kind.

Then her eyes rested on the silver pitcher she'd pulled out of the china cabinet for her special dinner. It was only a foot away from her on the table.

Beatrice still wanted to defuse the situation if she could. Or at least stall Julia.

"I figured you were being blackmailed by Henrietta, but it wasn't what I was imagining at first, was it? When I was at the library this morning, I talked to the librarian there. She was telling me that Henrietta was a frequent visitor. Apparently, she used the computer there a lot," said Beatrice.

Julia said tartly, "I wouldn't have thought that Henrietta had the brains or the tech-savvy not to use her own computer for her nastiness. I guess she must have been watching a lot of police shows on TV."

"All the time, I was thinking she was blackmailing you because of the painkillers," said Beatrice.

Noo-noo continued growling.

Julia said in a menacing voice, still keeping an eye on the corgi, "I told you I didn't care about people knowing about those pills. There are lots of people in the same situation."

"But you did care about your blog, didn't you? It wasn't only a big source of income, it was more. I got the impression the last time I spoke with you that you were very *proud* of it. That you got a real sense of creative fulfillment from blogging. And here was this troll who kept commenting on your blog posts. Kept saying that your marriage wasn't stable and that your husband, Jim, was having an affair."

"How did you find out about that?" hissed Julia.

"It wasn't easy," admitted Beatrice. "It wasn't something that the whole town knew about."

"Who else knows?" demanded Julia, brandishing the knife at Beatrice again.

Noo-noo barked sharply, snapping her jaws at Julia in the process.

Even as distracted as Beatrice was, she noticed that the smell of smoke was growing. She certainly wasn't about to give Miss Sissy's name over to Julia and have her be the next victim. She moved on: "But you knew it was Henrietta all along, even though she used a fake name on your blog. That's because she was using the comments to put pressure on you. So you slipped out from the quilt show. Did you actually plan on killing her when you went over there? I'm guessing that maybe you planned on just talking things through with Henrietta—to try to reason with her. After all, you'd been quilting together for years."

"You thought wrong," said Julia, her eyes glittering. "I knew Henrietta well enough by that point to realize that she would *never* listen. She was like a dog with a bone and stubborn as all get-out. What's more, she was just plain greedy and mean on top of it all. I'd already tried scaring her off with the email I sent to all the quilters and she couldn't have cared less. No, I may have gotten her to let me in by *saying* I wanted to talk with her, but I was looking for a way to get rid of her."

"I didn't think there were too many weapons in Henrietta's house. You didn't bring anything with you, just in case?" Beatrice now smelled a strong smell of burning and Noo-noo was looking concerned and sniffing the air wafting from the kitchen.

Julia said, "I figured there was something I could use there. It had to happen. She'd already tried to blackmail me about the painkillers, with little success. Then she wanted to try to blackmail me over the affair."

"She realized that's what you cared most about—the appearance of a happy married couple on your blog. So you ... what? Shoved her and then shoved the heavy sewing machine on top of her?" asked Beatrice.

"I figured if I needed to finish her off, there was a fire poker nearby," said Julia coolly. "And I wiped down any of my fingerprints from the machine. That took a few minutes. I knew my fingerprints were elsewhere in her house, but that could be easily explained since I was a visitor there sometimes."

Beatrice said, "Your husband's affair was with Minerva, wasn't it?"

Julia's grip was tight enough on the knife for her knuckles to be white. "I blame Minerva for that. She was the one who was pursuing Jim, not the other way around."

Beatrice remembered that Julia had not been with her husband at Minerva's funeral. He'd probably wanted to lie low.

"Minerva knew that you'd killed Henrietta. Her house was right next door to Henrietta's, after all. Regardless of what she told me or the police, she did leave the quilt show early enough to see you leaving Henrietta's house," continued Beatrice, taking a deep steadying breath.

"And I saw her. I could tell, by the way she acted around me that the guilt was getting to her," muttered Julia.

"Guilt?" asked Beatrice.

"Yes. And not the guilt she *should* be feeling! She wasn't guilty about having an affair with my husband—she was guilty knowing I got rid of Henrietta and that she wasn't telling the police about it! At first I thought she felt bad enough about the affair that she wouldn't say anything about my leaving Henrietta's house after the murder. After all, she didn't want *her* husband to know anything about the affair, either. Benjamin makes a lot of money and I don't think Minerva liked the idea of getting a divorce. But I saw her talking to Ramsay at Henrietta's funeral. I got as close as I could and I could tell she was saying she wanted an appointment to talk to him. I made sure she never got to that appointment."

Beatrice said in a tight voice, "And you knew exactly how to do that, because you knew Minerva's schedule."

"*Everyone* knew Minerva's schedule." Julia rolled her eyes.

"You knew she would be at the park on Saturday morning, filling feeders. You arrived early, maybe parking in another area and walking over so that your car wouldn't be seen at the park," said Beatrice.

"Aren't you smart?" sneered Julia.

"Then you scouted out a spot where you wouldn't be seen and hid in the woods until Minerva was absorbed in her task," said Beatrice. "Did she even know you were there?"

Julia said, "No. Believe me, she got off easy. Never knew what hit her. It was the perfect day. No one was there, for some reason. I did spot Hazel there with that dog of hers, but her idea of a walk isn't very strenuous and she left almost as soon as she got there. It was just as quiet as it could be. Just some guy fishing, and he looked half-asleep."

"And you brought a wrench with you," said Beatrice, feeling slightly sick as she said it. She was facing a woman who killed a friend with a wrench. The same woman was facing her now, with a knife. And Beatrice was no friend of hers.

"The wrench did an excellent job," said Julia. "Maybe a better job than this knife will do. If only you hadn't been so nosy, Beatrice! I bet I understand you better than you understand yourself. Let me guess. You moved here from the big city, right? You definitely have that big city feel about you. You thought you were coming to this idyllic place. Maybe it *was* an idyllic place for you. But you got a little bored. Not enough intellectual stimulation. So you played a very dangerous game to alleviate your boredom. And now you're going to pay."

But at that second, right as Julia lunged forward with the knife, Noo-noo's barks became higher pitched and more urgent and the smoke detector started shrilly going off.

Julia swung her head around to gape in the direction of the kitchen where smoke was now visible. Beatrice grabbed the heavy silver pitcher, full of ice, and swung it at Julia's head.

And Julia dropped like a rock, ice cubes scattering around her.

There was a frantic pounding on the front door as someone pushed through it. Wyatt's face was white with fear and confusion as his gaze took in smoke, Julia lying on the floor, the frantic corgi, and the silver pitcher. "Are you all right?"

Beatrice ran to him, hugged him briefly and fiercely and then said, "The kitchen!"

The pan and burner on the stove were both on fire and there was a lot of smoke billowing from the oven. Wyatt grabbed the kitchen fire extinguisher from a countertop and put out the flames on the burner. Beatrice grimaced at the pork chop. So much for supper.

They checked the oven and found the other pork chop incinerated, but no fire inside.

Wyatt said grimly, "Keep the extinguisher handy and let me know if the fire isn't completely out. I'll keep an eye on Julia. I'm assuming she— ?"

Beatrice nodded. "Julia is the killer. She's only knocked unconscious. We should call for help." Her head was starting to pound and she put up a hand to her forehead.

Wyatt gently reached out to hug her. "I'll call Ramsay. And the volunteer fire department for good measure."

Beatrice gave a shaky laugh. "And maybe the pizza delivery number, while you're at it." She stared ruefully at the smoky kitchen.

Noo-noo, who had followed them to the kitchen door to support them, looked sorrowfully at the disaster in the kitchen. Beatrice found her a couple of treats. "Good girl," she said. "You were helping too, weren't you?"

Noo-noo quickly ate the treats and then hearing something, turned to the front door, hearing something. In came Meadow and Ramsay with the same astonished looks on their faces that Wyatt had when he came in. Meadow was clutching the philodendron.

Meadow's eyes were huge as she took in the sight of Wyatt standing over a still-unconscious Julia. Ramsay quickly recovered and walked briskly over to Julia, bending down to check her.

"Will she be all right?" asked Beatrice.

"She's out like a light, but already stirring a little. We'll get her to the hospital to have her checked out before taking her in," said Ramsay. "Let me call Lieutenant Thomas to update him and then I'll want to talk with you."

Meadow peered sadly into Beatrice's kitchen. "I did find the white wine vinegar. I texted you about it, but you didn't answer. I started worrying that your recipe might be too much for you and so I got Ramsay to drop by on our way out to dinner. He and I were going to celebrate because one of those wrinkled old short stories is actually going to be published in a literary mag. I remembered to bring your plant back to you, too. But it looks as if your pork chops won't see any benefit from the vinegar."

"No, the pork chops are beyond anyone's help now," said Beatrice. She suddenly felt the need to sit down and shakily pulled out a chair at the table.

Wyatt walked over as Ramsay made his calls. He quietly put a soft quilt around Beatrice's shoulders and she smiled up at him. It must be the shock that made her cold, since she'd just been in a kitchen that was hot as the blazes from the oven.

Wyatt looked at the philodendron, still on the table where Meadow had absently stuck it. "Is that the houseplant I gave you?"

Beatrice gave a short laugh. "The very one. It went over to rehab at Meadow's house. Apparently I have the same type of talent with houseplants that I have with cooking."

Meadow briskly opened windows and the back door to let the smoky air out. She appeared to be furious, giving darting, angry looks at Julia. Ramsay gave her a wary look as he wrapped up his conversation with Lieutenant Thomas.

"Now, Meadow, settle down. And back away from Julia. Your menacing looks are worrying me," said Ramsay.

"Oh, I'm not going to do anything to Julia. I want her to rot miserably in jail for the next twenty years or more. I'm just so ... angry!" Meadow seethed.

Wyatt said with an understanding smile, "How about if you walk Noo-noo a bit?"

Beatrice said, "Please do! The poor thing. She was so stressed out. I'm sure she'd love a walk to relax a little."

Meadow looked relieved to have a mission of some kind. "Okay, that sounds good. I'll walk her downtown and back— that'll really stretch her legs and de-stress her."

As Meadow left, Ramsay muttered, "It'll stretch *Meadow's* legs and de-stress *her*, too! Sorely needed." He sighed. "It's never good when a quilter is a killer."

"But unfortunately, it wasn't much of a surprise in this case. Still, it's got to be hard for Meadow to wrap her head around," said Beatrice.

Ramsay spent a few minutes taking notes as Beatrice outlined everything that had happened. Wyatt stood by, looking grim as he heard the story.

Ramsay said, "Funny that she cared more that the illusion of the perfect marriage stay intact than she cared that her painkiller habit was revealed."

"Henrietta finally got to her. Once Henrietta started pressuring her by commenting publicly on her blog, Julia decided she had to go. After that, Julia needed to cover up her crime so she had to get rid of Minerva, who'd seen Julia leave Henrietta's house," said Beatrice. She watched as Julia began stirring on the floor as the sound of a siren approached.

"That's right. Meadow was always having covered dish suppers with Julia. Long ago, they'd play canasta or hearts together. And then there was always a quilt show or bee they'd be at. But Meadow will move past it. It may just take some time." Ramsay moved slightly out of the way as the EMTs entered.

"I'm going to need to go in the back of the ambulance with this one," he told them.

Suddenly, a particularly wild-looking Miss Sissy tore into the house. "What is it? Who is hurt?"

Beatrice realized that the sirens and ambulance must have scared her to death.

"It's okay, Miss Sissy," said Wyatt soothingly. "Beatrice is fine. It's Julia. She ... well, she needs a doctor."

The EMTs looked askance at the old woman, who was now edging closer to their patient.

"Evilll," she hissed.

Wyatt quickly invited her into the kitchen to have some non-charred food.

After Ramsay had left in the ambulance and Wyatt and Miss Sissy had settled in the living room, Beatrice looked sadly at Wyatt. "Once again, something has gotten in the way of our date."

He reached out and gave her a warm hug that lasted a full minute before giving her a tender kiss. "The only thing that matters is that you're safe."

Miss Sissy was watching them with laser focus. Beatrice attempted to pretend the old woman wasn't there.

"Unfortunately, our nice supper is in cinders," said Beatrice with a wry smile.

"I'm sure it was something very tasty, too," said Wyatt.

"It was impossible to tell *what* it was, isn't it? With the fire and the smoke and then the fire extinguisher foam? In a prior, happier, life, our supper was pork chops," said Beatrice with a sigh.

Wyatt said, "One of my favorite things. That was sweet of you to cook it."

Miss Sissy muttered to herself and ate some more Gouda cheese.

"I would say let's head out to a restaurant, but the truth is that I'm completely exhausted." Beatrice sank down onto her sofa and put her feet up on the coffee table. And Miss Sissy, who was continuing to eat, was probably working on eliminating the remainder of the food she had in the house.

"Of course you are. We'll figure out another day," said Wyatt.

Miss Sissy polished off her plate and barked at Wyatt, "Ride home?"

Beatrice said, "Do you really need one? You galloped over here very efficiently, I noticed." You could see Miss Sissy's house from Beatrice's front porch.

"Wrenched my ankle," said Miss Sissy succinctly.

"I'd be happy to drive you home," said Wyatt.

Meadow tapped lightly on the door and came in with Noo-noo. Both of them looked a good deal more relaxed. Noo-noo grinned at her as she trotted toward Beatrice and leaned against her leg.

Meadow said, "I could drive you home, Miss Sissy. Since Ramsay left in an ambulance, the car is still outside."

Miss Sissy scowled at Meadow. "No! Wyatt."

Meadow shrugged and gave a laugh. "Have it your way, Miss Sissy."

Wyatt asked Meadow, "How will Ramsay get back home from the hospital in Lenoir? I didn't even think about that."

"Oh, one of the policemen from the state police will give him a ride. He won't need me to." Meadow said. She looked at Beatrice with tears brimming in her eyes. "When I think what could have happened ...."

"Please don't," said Beatrice crisply. "I don't want to really think about it, either. At least it's all over and done and now justice can start its process."

"And we'll leave you to get some rest," said Wyatt. His quiet voice was somehow effective with Meadow, who certainly had looked prepared to stay for a while and rehash the case.

"Tomorrow," she said to Beatrice. "Tomorrow we'll talk."

"And so will we," said Wyatt, smiling at Beatrice.

Chapter Eighteen

The next day started late for Beatrice and Noo-noo, who found themselves sleeping in. In fact, it was so late when Beatrice woke up that she was startled at how high the sun was in the sky.

After taking Noo-noo out and feeding her, Beatrice looked to see what food Miss Sissy had left behind the night before. There were eggs in the fridge, but then she looked back at her stove and groaned. She didn't *immediately* feel like cleaning up the huge amount of dried chemicals that the fire extinguisher had left behind. She imagined the task was going to involve rubber gloves and both sweeping and vacuuming, plus damp paper towels. Beatrice frowned and looked over at her paper towel holder. She certainly didn't have nearly enough to tackle the job.

A few minutes later, she was headed to downtown Dappled Hills to the 'breakfast-all-day' restaurant for scrambled eggs, sausage links, hash browns, and a side order of grits.

Her cell phone chimed and Beatrice saw that it was Meadow.

"Where are you?" demanded Meadow when Beatrice answered the phone. "I'm at your house and I see your car is gone. I can't believe you even had the energy to get out of bed!"

Beatrice took a sip of her coffee and said, "Oh, I had the energy to get out of bed. I just didn't have the energy to clean off my stove so that I could make breakfast. I'm at Hens Restaurant, getting something to eat. I made sure to close the door to the kitchen so Noo-noo wouldn't be able to get in there and into that foam mess."

"I can completely understand. What a horror! I'll see you whenever you get back, no worries. Take your time," said Meadow hurriedly.

Beatrice did. In fact, she had a couple of refills of her coffee and somehow even managed to eat a fluffy biscuit after the huge breakfast she'd already consumed. While she was there, Piper called in to check on her.

"I saw your car was gone when I was heading out. How are you doing this morning?" she asked, a note of worry in her voice.

Beatrice said solidly, "I'm completely fine, Piper, believe me. I just ate a ton of food and am about to head back home. I'd much rather hear about how things are going for *you*."

The worry immediately left Piper's voice. "It's going really well! Ash and I have plans for a nice, relaxing dinner in a few nights. We've talked a lot about the type of wedding we want and the word that comes to mind most is 'intimate.' We want it to be a joyful celebration with our closest friends and family."

Beatrice felt relieved. She didn't think that Piper would want a fancy or over-the-top wedding, but it was good to hear it confirmed. "I love that idea. How are you and Ash planning to get that intimate feel?"

"I love what Wyatt's sister, Harper, did for her wedding: incorporating quilts in the church and at the reception. Since quilting makes me happy and so many of my friends happy, I thought having quilts as part of our day would help make it even more meaningful for me."

"I'm sure the Village Quilters would be honored for you and Ash to borrow quilts for the ceremony and reception. And I'd love for you to use some of my quilts, if you can handle the imperfections," said Beatrice wryly.

"Your quilts are beautiful, and you know it. Of course I want them! If we've got quilts from you and our friends, then it will be as if we're really making everyone we love part of our day, too."

"Miss Sissy has some gorgeous old quilts, you know. She could probably cover the entire church with them. I think some of them were even her mothers. This all sounds like a wonderful idea," said Beatrice. "It's going to be a beautiful service. Have you had a chance to talk with Wyatt about a date?"

"I did briefly talk with him on the phone, and he has a good number of open dates at the church for a wedding," said Piper. "And he was so happy for us! He's really such a kind, warm man."

"Sounds like you've been able to talk with Wyatt more than I have," said Beatrice ruefully.

Piper said, "I know. I felt bad about last night for *many* reasons, but one of them is that your nice evening with Wyatt had to be scrapped. And not for the first time, either." She paused. "Were you going to try to reschedule for tonight? Am I keeping you?"

"Oh, no. No, there's plenty of time today for me to call Wyatt and see what his schedule looks like. After last night, I'm definitely taking it easy today, aside from scrubbing my kitchen out. Besides, I love the distraction of talking about your wedding—it keeps me from thinking about the horrid mess I've got waiting for me to clean up. Wyatt and I will surely talk today to plan something. Although lately, planning something has apparently been the kiss of death. Maybe we just need to do something completely spontaneous to break the curse," said Beatrice with a sigh.

"Maybe so," said Piper. "All right, I should probably go now. I just wanted to check up on you and then I ended up talking about the wedding the whole time! Thanks for your ideas. Let me know if I can do anything."

"I will. I love you."

Beatrice finished up her breakfast, paid, and drove back home. When she pulled into her driveway, she saw that Meadow was there. What's more, Meadow appeared to have let herself in. She'd asked Meadow and Ramsay to take care of Noo-noo for her a month ago while she took a quick trip to Atlanta to visit old friends. But it was certainly unusual otherwise for Meadow to let herself into Beatrice's house.

When Beatrice opened the door, she saw Noo-noo grinning at her, a couple of treats in front of her. Meadow was also grinning at her: wearing some industrial-looking kitchen gloves and cleaning the last remaining bits of fire extinguisher foam off the stove. In Beatrice's dish drainer were the formerly-charred and now-gleaming pans from the night before. In addition, Meadow appeared to have mopped the floor and scrubbed her counters and switched out her kitchen towels for clean ones.

Beatrice felt strong emotions welling up in her and quickly hugged the surprised Meadow, who seemed a little uncomfortable with Beatrice's gratitude.

"Oh, it's nothing," said Meadow. "Pish! Have I ever shared with you that one of my favorite things to do is really *clean*? Scrub, I mean. There's nothing more satisfying, is there? You get an immediate result. Sometimes I'll even take before and after pictures of what I've cleaned, just to gloat."

"Meadow, thank you so much for this. I can't tell you how much I was dreading coming back home and spending the morning cleaning. Because I have a feeling it would take a lot longer for me to clean that mess up than it took you to do it."

Meadow waved off any further conversation about the miraculous transformation of Beatrice's kitchen. "No, no. Now I know you probably had coffee at breakfast, but I've brought over some dessert coffee and half-and-half. This stuff is positively sinful, it's so good. Let's have some over in your living room. I'll fill you in on what Ramsay told me this morning."

Before Beatrice knew it, she was sitting in her living room, Noo-noo curled contentedly at her feet, and a cup of coffee in her hand.

Meadow quickly finished cleaning up, washed her hands, and joined Beatrice. She said, "I'm not going to be here for too long, because I promised I'd help Ash with a couple of wedding-related errands. But I wanted to make sure I checked in with you and made sure that you were all right. What a dreadful night last night! At least now everything is finally back to normal."

"What did Ramsay find out?" asked Beatrice.

"Oh, that Julia confessed to everything. That's the only decent thing the woman has done since this whole mess started. And it was all above-board, of course. Ramsay recommended that she get a lawyer, although Julia apparently didn't seem much interested. She was ready to get it all off her chest. Still, they did get one for her and the lawyer did her best to get Julia to keep her mouth closed," said Meadow.

Beatrice said, "But Julia kept on talking?"

"Ramsay said she seemed to want to get it over with. So she gave him all the details about Henrietta's and Minerva's deaths— why she'd killed them, how she'd gone about it, etc. It's amazing to me that Julia would be so violent over that blog of hers," said Meadow, shaking her head.

"I think she didn't want to lose that book deal," said Beatrice. "And she didn't want all her blog readers to think that her 'happy marriage' was a sham. At any rate, it's all over now. And at least we know that justice will be carried out."

"What I didn't understand is how you *knew* what had happened and why Julia was determined to get rid of you, too," said Meadow. Her brow was furrowed.

"Honestly, Julia simply misinterpreted something that I said. I saw her at the library before the funeral. I asked her about Henrietta coming to the library every day and then I made some offhand comment about Ramsay giving me so much to read that *I* didn't need to come to the library for a while, or some such thing."

Meadow gasped. "So Ramsay's short stories nearly got you killed! That Ramsay."

"Well, indirectly. Julia thought I was threatening her—that I knew something. Maybe she even thought I'd blackmail her over the information like Henrietta had," said Beatrice.

"But *did* you know it was Julia then?" asked Meadow impatiently. "Could you tell while you were at the library? Did you give yourself away and *that's* why she came after you later?"

"Not at all. I'd like to *say* that I knew it was Julia then, but the truth is that I suspected her just as much as everyone else. But when I saw her at my door, I knew. Even though Julia was probably prepared to pass off her appearance at my house as a visit, I realized she was the killer." Beatrice took a sip of her coffee to warm herself up after feeling that cold certainty course through her again.

"But *how*? I had no idea and I had the same information that you did," said Meadow.

"The fact that Henrietta was at the library and that *Julia* was also at the library when I was talking to her was probably the trigger. Henrietta was using the library's computers so that no one could trace her computer. The person who was the troll on Julia's site wouldn't have wanted to be traced if Julia reported harassing comments. Seeing *Julia* at the library reminded me of her blog and also made me wonder if Julia had been the one who hacked Posy's email and sent out the message about Henrietta," said Beatrice.

Meadow sighed. "Well, that's smart of you. I don't think those things would have occurred to me."

"It wasn't only that. In a flash, I also thought about what Miss Sissy had said about Minerva having an affair. I saw June Bug yesterday afternoon and she told me that Jim and Minerva had acted very close while in her shop. It seemed very likely that Minerva's affair was with Julia's husband. Julia's blog offered a glimpse at an allegedly happy and rewarding marriage. She got a book deal because of this illusion. Julia wouldn't have wanted news of an affair to leak out. It might even have made the publisher decide to back out of the book contract."

"So Julia walked over here with a knife," said Meadow in a deeply angry voice.

"She did. But she didn't pull the knife out at once. Julia just suspected that I knew something and decided to come over to probe a little more," said Beatrice.

"Why did you even let her in?" fretted Meadow.

"She pushed her way in. Besides, I was thinking it was Wyatt, running a bit early for supper. Or maybe you with a bottle of wine vinegar after all," said Beatrice. "But once I saw Julia and realized she was the killer, *she* knew that *I* knew. At that point, she was ready to get rid of me, too."

"Well thank heaven that you burned supper to a crisp," said Meadow.

"I know. The smoke detector going off and Noo-noo going berserk created the perfect distraction," said Beatrice.

"Sweet, brave Noo-noo," said Meadow fondly. She reached over to rub the little dog and then stood briskly up, picking up her coffee cup and heading to the kitchen. "All right, I've got to head out to meet up with Ash," she said as she busily hand-washed her cup. "Do you think you can go back to sleep?"

"I'm pretty sure I *can't*. But I'm putting my feet up," said Beatrice.

"That's good. I talked to Piper this morning and we agreed that you need a very quiet late-morning and afternoon!" Meadow threw Beatrice a kiss. "Hope that you and Noo-noo can take it easy."

A couple of hours after Meadow left, Piper surprised her by ordering lunch to be delivered to her house from one of her favorite cafés in Dappled Hills. Beatrice ate up the broccoli and cheese soup in the sourdough bread bowl and the delicious chopped chef salad that came with it.

Beatrice discovered that she actually *could indeed* take a nap. She fell asleep on the sofa and Noo-noo snored gently beside her for the better part of an hour. Then she spent time reading Ramsay's stories, which surprised her by being far better than she had expected.

It was suppertime when Beatrice's cell phone buzzed at her. She hoped it was Wyatt, trying to reschedule their dinner for the umpteenth time. She squinted at her phone and sighed. It was a text message from Miss Sissy.

"Need ride," the text succinctly stated.

"Where are you?" responded Beatrice. She hadn't planned on going back out.

"At church." Miss Sissy was fond of running by the church to visit with Wyatt.

Beatrice texted back, "But you live close by! You usually walk!" Her use of excessive exclamation points was a testament to the fact that she was chagrined at going back out.

"Hip is cranky," read Miss Sissy's crisp reply.

Beatrice was already walking into her bedroom to put on her shoes, run a comb through her hair, and touch up her makeup. In Dappled Hills, whenever she left the house without makeup or without combing her hair, she always saw every person she knew in the town.

"All right," texted Beatrice. "I'll be there in five minutes."

"K. Will wait inside."

"Why not outside?" asked Beatrice. "I'll be right there! You could wait outside."

Miss Sissy stubbornly texted, "Sitting down."

Beatrice groaned in frustration, grabbed her car keys, gave Noo-noo a pat, and left. The only thing good about this was that at least Miss Sissy wasn't driving herself around. She was a menace to society when she did. Miss Sissy was very fond of driving on sidewalks.

Beatrice pulled up to the old church, appreciating once again how it seemed to blend in with the nature surrounding it. Its stones were moss and ivy-covered, and the building was surrounded by flowering trees and bushes. She always felt calmer when she was here.

She parked out front and hesitated. Where *exactly* 'inside' was Miss Sissy? In the sanctuary? In the Sunday school building? Or in one of the other areas of the church? Beatrice walked down the brick walkway that led to a few steps at the front of the church and pushed open the wooden doors that led to the sanctuary.

She walked into the dim room, with its arched ceiling and beautiful old wood that was lovingly polished to gleam. "Miss Sissy?" she called, wincing as her voice echoed around the sanctuary. Clearly, no one was here. Even if Miss Sissy had fallen asleep in the brief interval before Beatrice arrived, she'd have heard that echoing call.

She walked down the aisle to the doors leading out to the rest of the church. She walked down halls laid with red carpet, past empty Sunday school rooms. "Miss Sissy?" called Beatrice, feeling exasperated. Miss Sissy *had* said the church, not Wyatt's house.

After a couple of minutes, she reached the church's formal dining room, which she peered into. Nothing but a room of tables set up for the next church dinner.

Finally, she opened the door to the church's smaller, more intimate dining room across the hall. And caught her breath.

Wyatt was standing inside, smiling tenderly at her. Candles were lit on each of the small, round tables covered with starched white tablecloths, and on each table were freshly-picked flowers of all sorts in church vases. There were also flowers on the sideboards, which seemed to be loaded with delicious-smelling foods—shrimp pasta, vegetable casserole, mixed fruits, and pies.

"Wyatt?" asked Beatrice, barely able to speak.

That's when Wyatt dropped to one knee. "Beatrice, would you do me the great honor of marrying me?"

Beatrice gave a gasping laugh. "I will. I will, Wyatt."

And the next few minutes were spent in silence.

Minutes later, Wyatt had Beatrice, glowing with happiness, sit in one of the ancient wooden chairs where he served her a feast.

"Wyatt," she said with a laugh, "have you been cooking all day? You're putting my poor pork chops to shame."

"I have a confession," he said, eyes twinkling. "Piper knew I was going to ask you and she wanted to cook, too. So the food is from both of us, with love."

"*Piper* knew? She keeps a secret better than I knew," said Beatrice, watching as Wyatt filled her plate with shrimp pasta.

"She's known for a while," admitted Wyatt. "And she helped me pick all the flowers here from our yards and some off the church grounds."

Beatrice's eyes opened wide. "Oh! You've been trying to propose all this time?" She covered her mouth with her hand. She thought of Piper following up with her, asking her whether she'd planned another date with Wyatt. Thought of her consternation that the previous dinners and picnic hadn't gone as planned.

"It just took a while longer than expected, through no fault of our own," said Wyatt.

"And Miss Sissy? She was obviously part of the plot, too," said Beatrice.

"Miss Sissy was apparently listening in very closely last night. When I took her home, she demanded that we have our dinner tonight instead of waiting any longer. She told me that she wanted to help. And we'd had such bad luck when we *planned* for dinner that the spontaneous approach with Miss Sissy giving a trumped up excuse seemed like a better way." Wyatt grinned at her as he helped his own plate. "She picked some of the flowers, too."

"I didn't even know Miss Sissy *had* flowers," said Beatrice, thinking of the little house covered with vines like something out of Sleeping Beauty. She wondered where Miss Sissy had picked them. "Everything is so beautiful."

"May I say a blessing? I've got so much to be thankful for," said Wyatt, his voice wavering a little.

And as he blessed their food and their lives together, sitting in that candlelit church dining room that was brightened with flowers from her family and friends, Beatrice had never felt more loved in her life.

About the Author:

Elizabeth writes the Southern Quilting mysteries and Memphis Barbeque mysteries for Penguin Random House and the Myrtle Clover series for Midnight Ink and independently. She blogs at ElizabethSpannCraig.com/blog, named by Writer's Digest as one of the 101 Best Websites for Writers. Elizabeth makes her home in Matthews, North Carolina, with her husband and two teenage children.

Sign up for Elizabeth's **free newsletter** to stay updated on releases (and for favorite easy recipes):

http://eepurl.com/kCy5j

Other Works by the Author:

Myrtle Clover Series in Order:
Southern Quilting Mysteries in Order:
Memphis Barbeque Mysteries in Order (Written as Riley Adams):
And a standalone "cozy zombie" novel: Race to Refuge, written as Liz Craig

Acknowledgments

I've written more than twenty books, which makes me think of all the help I've had along the way. This help started with my parents and grandmothers back in the 70s and 80s. They read to me and encouraged my early writing.

My teachers also played a huge role in encouraging me. My second grade teacher, Mrs. Thomas, first introduced the thought of writing as a career to me. My fourth grade teacher, Penny Tritt, played the biggest role in encouraging me, even after I went on to other grades.

The online writing community, quick to offer resources and support, has been a tremendous help to me from 1997 on.

My husband and children are proud of me and tell others about my work.

Karri Klawiter is my cover designer and always seems to know just what I want in a cover.

My mother, Beth Spann, a fast and savvy reader who always tells me when the story gets confusing. Amanda Arrieta, who knows my characters so well and what they would or wouldn't do. Dan Harris, a careful reader with helpful corrections. Judy Beatty is my cheerful and kind editor.

And Sandra Harding, my original editor at Penguin, who helped me originally develop these characters and stories.

Where to Connect With Elizabeth:

Facebook: Elizabeth Spann Craig Author
Twitter: @elizabethscraig
Website: elizabethspanncraig.com
Email: mailto:elizabethspanncraig@gmail.com

Thanks!

Thanks so much for reading my book...I appreciate it. If you enjoyed the story, would you please leave a short review on the site where you purchased it? Just a few words would be great. Not only do I feel encouraged reading them, but they also help other readers discover my books. Thank you!

Extras:

Interested in having a character named after you? In a Myrtle Clover tote bag? Or even just your name listed in the acknowledgments of a future book? Visit my Patreon page at https://www.patreon.com/elizabethspanncraig

CPSIA information can be obtained
at www.ICGtesting.com
Printed in the USA
LVOW10s2343171017
552827LV00008B/137/P